THE LEGACY SERIES

Finding the Bones: Stories & A Novella
Nikki Kallio

Self-Defense
Corey Mertes

Where Are Your People From?
James B. De Monte

Sometimes Creek
Steve Fox

The Plagues
Joe Baumann

The Clayfields
Elise Gregory

Kind of Blue
Christopher Chambers

Evangelina Everyday
Dawn Burns

Township
Jamie Lyn Smith

Responsible Adults
Patricia Ann McNair

Great Escapes from Detroit
Joseph O'Malley

Nothing to Lose
Kim Suhr

The Appointed Hour
Susanne Davis

AN INSTINCT

FOR MOVEMENT

LINKED STORIES

MICHAEL MATTES

CORNERSTONE PRESS
UNIVERSITY OF WISCONSIN-STEVENS POINT

Cornerstone Press, Stevens Point, Wisconsin 54481
Copyright © 2024 Michael Mattes
www.uwsp.edu/cornerstone

Printed in the United States of America by
Point Print and Design Studio, Stevens Point, Wisconsin

Library of Congress Control Number: 2024935799
ISBN: 978-1-960329-41-7

Cornerstone Press titles are produced in courses and internships offered by the Department of English at the University of Wisconsin–Stevens Point.

DIRECTOR & PUBLISHER
Dr. Ross K. Tangedal

EXECUTIVE EDITORS
Jeff Snowbarger, Freesia McKee

EDITORIAL DIRECTOR
Ellie Atkinson

SENIOR EDITORS
Brett Hill, Grace Dahl

PRESS STAFF
Logan Bidon, Sam Bjork, Jolie Chambers-Moffitt, Carolyn Czerwinski, Sophie McPherson, Eva Nielsen, Sthefanie Padilla, Ava Willett

For Katherine, Simon, and Kira

CONTENTS

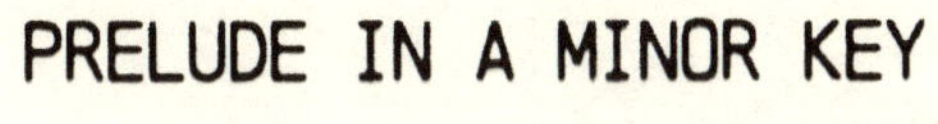

PRELUDE IN A MINOR KEY

WAYFINDER

A boy arrives home from school and retrieves a shovel from a garden chest, then walks a slow circuit around his family's property. He finds a shiner by the front door, half eaten, and a more or less intact vole beneath the dogwood out back. Using the shovel as a kind of oar, he flings the remains across the creek, then hoses off the spatter from the welcome mat.

If he reflects on this chore at all, one he performs every day, it is with a sense of his accountability in the matter, which he cannot think how to resolve. "Keep the butchery out of sight," his mother has warned, "or Smokey is off to the county rescue."

After stowing the shovel, he drifts back to the streambank and gazes at the purling water. The shiners are a recent development, and the strangeness of it gnaws at him. He knows every twist in this creek for a mile in both directions and has never come upon them, let alone anything of the size Smokey hauls in: sometimes eight or nine inches tip-to-tailfin he guesses, though it is impossible to say exactly, as Smokey invariably has what she cares to before making a gift of the rest.

"Saw that feline of yours take down a crow last week," old man McElwain calls out from the screened-in porch where he spends much of his time. "Could hardly believe the sight of it. Like she had an open umbrella in her teeth."

The boy glances toward the house next door and nods but doesn't say anything. He had found the crow and wondered how she managed it. Juncos and towhees and such he was accustomed to, but the crow was half her size.

"A crow in distress, that's like flying knives coming at you," McElwain says while maneuvering out onto the porch stoop. "She may not be so lucky next time." He grips the iron stair railing with both hands, puffs on his pipe from the corner of his mouth.

"You ever seen fish in the creek, Mr. Mac? Real fish, not just minnows?"

"Sure I have. Before the state diverted the headwaters and knocked out half the flow. Then Dupont set up shop here, and all these builder homes were acquired by chemists fond of dumping poison on their yards. Bringing their work home with them, you could say. It's a wonder there's a living thing in that brook with all the runoff."

He adds, after shifting his pipe from one side to the other, "Apologies to your father who is a man of the trades and can't be bothered to dote on his lawn."

The boy looks around to see if Smokey is in sight, but most times she isn't. The house has become a safehold for her, his mother says: a place to put up for a few days, bank some sleep, take in some easy meals, recover from a fight. Then she's off again.

"I'll be seeing you, Mr. Mac," the boy says and turns heel toward the kitchen door, realizing how hungry he is.

"Alright then," he hears over the low whoosh of the trees and moving water.

———

The boy sets out mid-morning the Sunday after, the air pale and stagnant. Working his way down the creek, he plinks over stepping-stones, crabwalks boulders, keeps his head low out of instinct, having been run off his share of backyards and farm fields. He climbs up to the high bank to skirt retaining walls or to dodge brambles and poison ivy. All the while he watches the water, holds his shadow close, tries not to roil the surface, knowing most creatures in this stream are shy.

An hour or so along, he reaches a three-lane boulevard where the creek tunnels under through a box culvert. He has rarely followed it this far and has never gone farther. The impulse to wade through is chased from his mind, as he is without a flashlight and has seen banded snakes in this water more than once. "Most of them are common northerns," old Mac has told him. "But there is the occasional cottonmouth."

He darts across the road and down to the drainage on the other side which funnels out to a narrow wood. There is a public pool to the east, closed until noon, and a church just to the west. He watches for a moment as families shuffle through the arched doorway, adults peering under crooked hands into the sunlight. A neighborhood kid, Jaime, slips into view, and he folds deeper into the leaf cover knowing Jaime would spot him if anyone could. He hadn't told him of his plans, nor anybody else, feeling somehow he mustn't. It is a notion he has taken into his head, that the mystery of the shiners is his and that the answer ought to be too.

As he continues farther south, the unfamiliarity of the terrain makes him newly alert to the movement and contours of the creek channel. He can tell where it flows wild and where it has been shaped to cut between homes, loop around a cul-de-sac, or make way for a parking lot. The rift in those sections seems plumbed, scoured, more ditch-like, in the manner of a trench that a machine would dig out. The natural parts wander, run this way and that, through flat, silty stretches; through jags of rockfall where the water boils.

At times he'll stop and observe, turn over stones, pass a stick under a snag, take a kind of census of the nooks and hollows that catch his eye. One spot will be barren, another full of life: minnows, crayfish, striders, swimming frogs, just like he finds near home. But the creek rarely deepens or fans out to an extent that a mature shiner would find hospitable.

He expects all along to be sniffed out by a dog and knows he's lucky he hasn't been. On a couple of occasions he spies adults gardening near the bank and lies back until they turn away. The shouts of kids playing break out intermittently from above, and while he hasn't encountered any in the creek bed, he has taken note of their handiwork: pails laid in the water for unlucky creatures to venture into; makeshift dams to prevent an escape.

Negotiating a swirling double bend, something makes him lift his gaze. Maybe thirty yards off, a girl stands barefoot in the stream, cupped hands held in front of her. He realizes she noticed him first, and the idea of it makes him wince. Struck by indecision, he takes a step in her direction, stops, pans around. The buffer to his left is wooded, its understory grown over by skunk cabbage. He could portage there, and he's thinking that he might. To his right are lawns and homes.

"Wanna see?" the girl calls out and raises her hands a little higher.

He drags his wrist across his forehead, seized by thirst, though he scarcely noticed it a moment earlier. How long has he been on the move? Three hours, maybe? The distance he has no sense of, though he reckons it has been miles. Didn't his father once tell him the creek runs all the way to the Delaware?

Without really deciding to, he steps along toward the girl. She is younger than he is—a couple grades behind, he guesses. She extends her upturned palms, and he sees she has a sallie there, squirming in curlicues, frantic to free itself. She lets him study it for a moment, then sets it gently on a rock, and they watch it shimmy into the water … so swift and so smooth, the surface zipped up behind it.

"I don't see those too much anymore," he says with a kind of hushed reverence, trying and failing to recall the last time he would've. He thinks back to what old Mac had said and grazes his fingertips over the surface. He has never had reason to regard that term, "runoff," but he's sure he understands what it means.

"Know where I can find some water?" he asks, and the girl smiles wide and points down. They both laugh.

He mimes drinking from a hose, and she scrambles up the bank and signals for him to follow. They gambol across the lawn to a spigot affixed to the house where he gulps his limit, plus as much as he can choke down for however much longer he'll need it. As he jogs back toward the creek, water running from his chin, a pointer appears out of nowhere and bolts in his direction. He leaps into the streambed and up the other side, then tears a swath through the cabbage into the shallow wood. When he is satisfied the chase is abandoned, he leans against a stump to catch his breath and to eject a slug of what he just drank. Staring emptily through the tree line to a road just beyond, he sees a car steer into a driveway and a family clamber out, the lot of them in dress-up like he noticed at the church.

Trying to order his thoughts, he wonders if he should quit and head home, but he can't sort out why he would or he wouldn't. He remembers the candy bar stuffed in his pocket but discovers it melted when he works it free. Full up with water, he has no great craving for it anyway.

Moving at an angle to the creek, he pokes into the clear several houses down. He stands up tall for a moment and peers back for the girl, but there is no girl, there is no dog. The current, to his eye, seems more interwoven here; awakens in him a wayfinding instinct, although he wouldn't recognize it as such. It is enough to send him onward.

The boy crosses his fifth laned road since setting off for the day, each time shunning the dark, concrete chutes that run below. An awareness that he's near his grandparents' street helps him situate where he is in relationship to home. He barely glances at the water as he skirrs along, other than to track its movement, its drift, the quest for shiners having at some point fallen from his consciousness. His only thought is to advance now, to echo the coursing of the creek as it searches for the river.

Feeling well rid of the stretch behind him, which was strewn with tires, shopping carts, beer cans, and other debris, he swallows the effusion of the woods, the mossy damp, the waft of decay from the humus underfoot. Fed by connecting runnels, the creek is wider and deeper here, its bottom a pit of shadows. Logs are laid across pinched sections to allow traverses between banks.

Emerging into a mown field, he hears someone yell, "Trespasser," followed by a blast of threats and harsh words. He keeps his sights set ahead of him, not caring anymore whose land he's on and figuring he can outrun any two legs attached to that voice, should the need arise.

Not long after exiting the tree cut, he detours a wide, teeming expanse of reeds and sedges. Finding his way back to the creek, he questions for a moment if he hasn't come upon an altogether separate body of water. Mottled with light, a vast, deep pool opens before him, its surface nearly motionless but for its unhurried glide beneath a railroad trestle.

He realizes in a rush that he has been here before; had followed his nose to this spot a year or two past, venturing out from his grandparents' rowhouse only a short distance away. The very same creek, the one in his backyard, miles down the line. He hadn't thought to wonder.

There'll be no going farther, he understands. Beyond the tracks is the freeway; a ways beyond that, the river; the route unpassable on foot, he is sure. Whether such certainty is born of acquired knowledge or a sudden keenness to see his grandparents, the boy is not given to contemplate.

He climbs a boulder that juts over the water, removes his sneakers, dangles his feet off the edge. A panic he hadn't known was inside him drains from his toes, slips away with the current. He lies flat against the cool granite, squints into the light tracing through the trees. The whirr of the interstate arrives in gusts, sounds to him like a river in flood. In his laughing mind he sees shiners, one after another, silvering in the torrent.

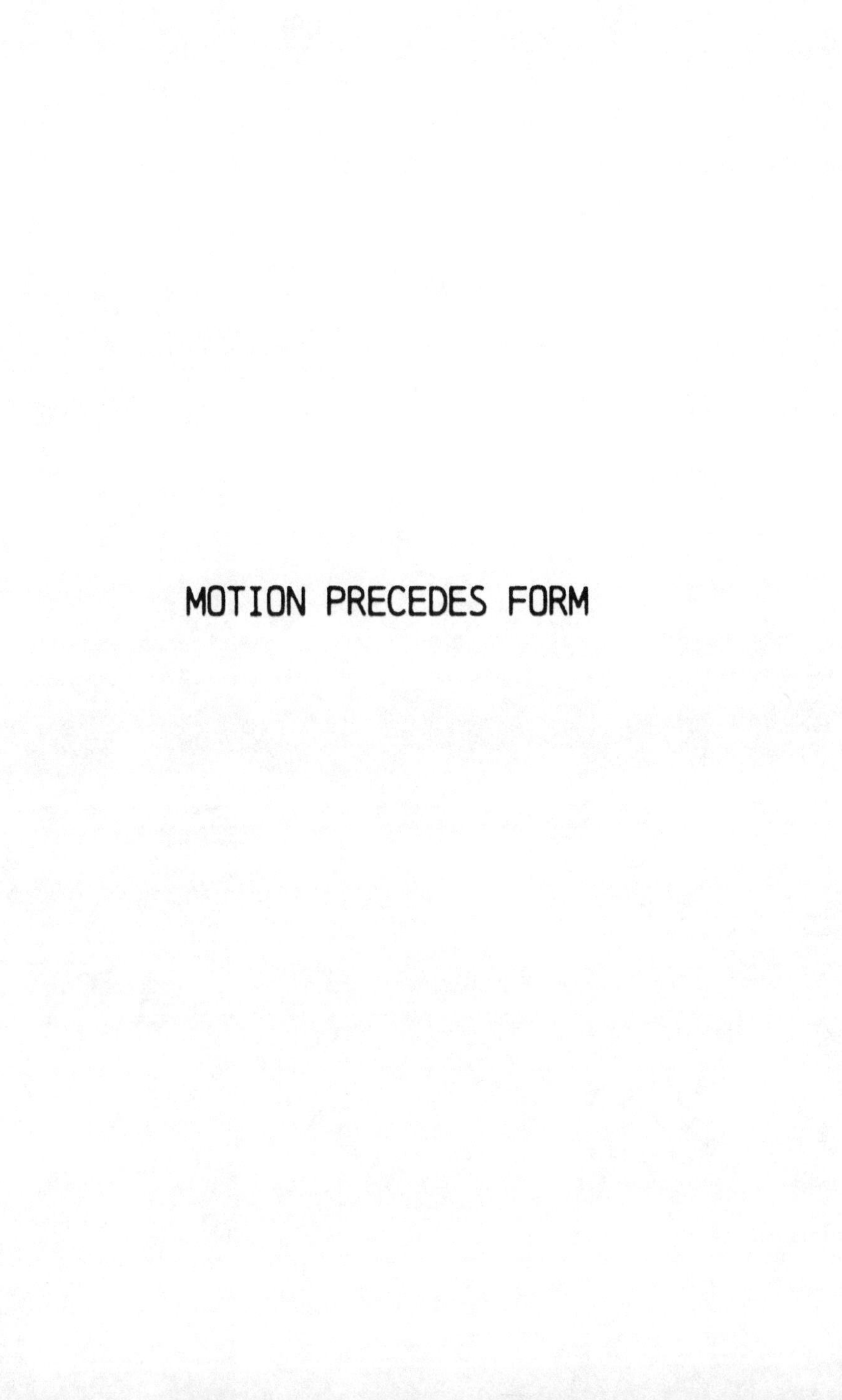

MOTION PRECEDES FORM

AN UNDIGNIFIED
NAME FOR A HORSE

At dawn on a day that would soon come to matter, in a house in a town I would then have to leave, I knelt for a moment on the second-floor landing and laced up my boots. It was quiet and yet it wasn't, the slam of the front door still shivering through the walls. Two thin panels of light shone up from the decorative glass on either side of the entryway, and I used these to guide myself down. I still clung to sleep, tried to remain as close to it as possible.

The car stood idling in the driveway, traces of an overnight shower beading along its drip rails. I could see him hunched behind the wheel, eyes closed, face hovering over an open flask of coffee, taking in his morning vapors. This grated on me, of course, as did every habit of his I took notice of. Never mind that I had caught myself around that time doing exactly the same thing with a bong.

I ducked in without saying anything and leaned my head against the window. The air in the car smelled like the inside of his mouth, a quality I knew well owing to his near constant presence in my face in those years. The gloomy ride across town only intensified the effect.

The trades park was quiet when we arrived, the machine yards and metal buildings not yet come to life. His shop didn't stand out in any particular way, just another site where trucks and laborers came and went. That often included me, though only on weekends that summer to service the fleet and only then because I needed the extra cash. The job I'd taken in the stockroom at Gaylord's accounted for most of my time. It just didn't pay enough.

There were six trucks in all, and in addition to regular oil changes, there were always plugs to replace, new distributor caps to pop on, and a few heavier repairs I might try to fake my way through. I had missed a couple of Saturdays that month, so there was plenty of work waiting for me. As he strode toward the office, he stopped and asked me to admire the new blacktop they poured during the week.

"It looks smooth," I told him.

"Don't spill any gas," he said. "When it's fresh like that, gas'll eat right through it."

It did look nice, and it reeked of tar and sealant, and it said something about the fortunes of the business I wouldn't otherwise have had reason to consider. I jumped in place a few times. It still had a little bounce.

I killed a few minutes walking the perimeter, toeing at the seams, dislodging a flake here and there. My throat was plugged and burning from the night before, so I knelt by the curb and tried to grind it out. Afterward I pulled a Coke from the machine and swigged from it while strolling around the trucks. Usually I'd get some vibe as to who wanted to go first. At one time or another I rode in all those trucks, over weekends, school holidays, summers, doing lackey work for the electricians. I knew them too damn well.

The best was Jimmy's, a smart tall-box dually that he kept so nice and clean. Jimmy was the senior guy, he babied his truck, and almost nothing ever went wrong with it.

Cale's rig, on the other hand, was the most disorganized dump-on-wheels imaginable. Pipe, couplings, wire reels, breakers, power tools, wrench sets, whatever, all lay in a heap on the floor. It created so much drag the tail end rode sunk in its haunches. That's worthwhile to visualize because Cale was the same way, humping around in his tool belt, pants hanging low, his floppy ass just barely off the ground. Who knows why, but that truck sipped oil like it would never get another drop. And there's a plug for Ford for you: it was nothing but an old Econoline van.

Of all the long-termers, I worked with Cale the most. Maybe twice in those years he used my name. Lapper, he called me. *Hey lapper, hand me those vise grips. Hey lapper, run a fish up that wall.* Hey lapper *this*, hey lapper *that*, all day long.

Next to Cale's stood Zando's wreck, or whatever was left of it by then. Zando was nearly deaf and couldn't hear the gears and tore through clutch after clutch. That truck truly hated Zando. It had no sensitivity for his disability. It was mistreated and resented it and was a bitch to even get near. It was always on Zando's truck that I'd chum my knuckles.

After draining the Coke, I backed out Cale's van. I spun twice around the block, then eased onto the pad. The ride felt like it always did, a disaster. The weight from the junk pile had buckled the suspension, and the engine ran as if it didn't give a damn. Plus, you could hardly feel the clutch engage. It moved in and out like … well, you know. I do have to watch my language. I picked that up from those guys all those years ago and have never been able to shake it. Tradesmen have filthy mouths, in general.

I slid a trap underneath the pan and torqued off the plug. While the oil drained, I swapped out the filter, then tapped open the lid to the reclamation drum. The spent oil ran red at the margins as I dumped it in. It was part of Cale's mystique, there was always that tinge, whether it had been one month or three. I looked over and the truck was kind of smirking at me while I was doing this. "Bite me," I said, remembering the time an axle dropped out on me on a donut run. *Go get me a jelly roll, lapper.*

I funneled in the fresh oil, gassed up, then went on to Jimmy's and then Dave's truck. I planned to leave Zando's for last but changed my mind and decided to get it out of the way. The engine whined badly as I pulled out, but that was someone else's problem, not mine. I'd heard him swear a hundred times to hell he'd fire Zando, that he cost more money than he brought in, and not only with the truck but with his constant fuckups on jobs. But go figure, the guy who was such a prick to his kids happened to have a heart when it came to drunks, down-and-outers, and all the other hard-up cases who tripped in there looking for work.

So I changed the oil—which was black and chunked out like a Slurpee might from a hole at the bottom of a cup—then jammed in the gas nozzle and set the clip. I walked to the back of the building and sat down on some tires. There were a few crumbs in my shirt pocket from wherever, so I slipped a paper from my wallet and rolled them in. It was a pitiful little boy, but I lit up anyway.

I have to guess some about the next few minutes, though I think I can do this pretty well. Several sad-sack row houses lined the alley behind the shop, and I probably looked out at these, into their backyards. Come summertime, there were always cage fans rattling in the windows, sheets and towels aflutter on clotheslines, a couple of thug dogs on patrol. I know it rained later that day, so I would've gazed up awhile and followed the clouds. We'd get these big, battleship-type clouds when a late-season storm was rolling in, and I loved watching them teeter across the sky. Of course, for the millionth time that summer, I'd have said to myself, "You've got to get out of here," but there wouldn't have been anything firm behind the thought. I didn't have enough money and, as it was, had continued to smoke away a lot of what I earned. I could've moved up the chain and sold a few ounces, people did hit me up on occasion, and it would've gone a long a way toward improving my finances. But I had done it a couple times before and it wasn't me. I just wanted to have my stash and be happy.

Only a blink away from nodding off, I heard a yell—a low, sustained, agonized yell. It was huge. It flumed and rang out and boomed through the early morning air. Every other sound fell away from it. I jumped up and bolted from out back, then froze as I rounded the corner of the building—just as he jerked the nozzle out of the truck. The clip had jammed. A wide slick of gas had run off the pad and onto the blacktop. He shouted again, then whipped around to face me.

I know it wasn't like this at the time, that it was fast and simple, a blur of reactions; yet now, in my mind, everything falls carefully into place. Everything that would come into play when the next move was made. Him. Me. Where he stood relative to me, the truck, the building, the fence, and the street. The push broom only a few feet away from him, hanging from a cleat bolted to the wall block. The prospect behind me, which was no prospect at all: the rear fence I was gazing through was rimmed with razor wire, and going over it was the only way out from the back of the property.

At once—at last—he reached for the push broom. I angled for the far corner of the driveway. If I got there first, I'd make it to the street, and then I'd be gone. But he moved fast, and as I skidded by he drew close enough to take a swing. I dove and the clout-end of the broom whirled over my head and back, then tore into the fence. The swing threw him off balance, and the broom, I think, somehow became lodged in the chain-link. Before he could regroup, I was up and running and in the street. I didn't have to but kept going hard for half a mile, all the way to the avenue.

I stopped there, dropped to my knees, tried to take in some air. It was a dank morning, and this was a sooty part of town, so doing this wasn't exactly rejuvenating. But the gunk in my chest finally dislodged in one great, dripping ball, and I was immediately better-off for it.

As I knelt there, studying my creation, watching it writhe and coddle, a car blazed the corner across from me and braked hard. I looked up. It was Cale. Cale coming in on a Saturday. For a second I had to assure myself I wasn't laid out back there on the asphalt, neck snapped, experiencing some kind of near-death delusion.

"Hey!" he called out. "There he is! Young Prince Nut Lapper. I hear you're stocking diapers at the mall this summer. That mean you've given up on being my boss someday?"

I don't recall what I said to him, if I said anything. I only remember what he looked like—looked like at that moment, my head still a can of cold atoms, my eyes full of bleary wind. His stupendously fat face hung out the window, spilled from both sides of his sleeveless shoulder. His thick tube of an arm dangled down the door panel from there. Hell, what else could I do? I walked straight over and gave him a long, soppy lick up his cheek.

A whack against the window frame—*Cale's head.* A streak of yelling and foul language—*Cale's voice.* I was aware of it but had already begun to walk away. Not run this time, walk, up the avenue, one of the only true hills in town.

I felt sorry, or, at least now, imagine I felt sorry, for Cale, the trucks, the shop, the street; the buildings I passed on the street. They were condemned in the way that things are when you know you'll never see them again.

Near the top of the rise, I stopped to retie my boots. A bus swung to the curb and its door opened. I glanced up the pole at my back and realized where I was standing. The driver's hand was on the lever and he gave me an on-or-off look. I shook my head, and as he trailed away I felt better, clearer. It was just the loose suggestion of it, that there would always be a ride to somewhere.

Veering north from the warehouse district, past the rail spurs, under the freeway, I came out into a dead zone of rubbled lots, the occasional hollowed-out structure not yet bulldozed. Like squared-off fields of broken chalk. Half of downtown had drifted into this state.

What he'd done ... rather, the near result to me of what he'd done was, I knew, or perhaps decided as I trekked along, not so exceptional. Everyone is almost dying. Almost dying, then walking away without a scratch. Chokings, car wrecks, near car wrecks, near drownings, small slips that stave fatal falls. Only a few days earlier, a deer rifle was leveled at me after the car I was in—not driving, just in—pancaked a mailbox. *Twice in a week, hell …*

It's possible, too, that he swung to miss or that he jerked up an inch on some restraining impulse. Years had passed since he had really come after me, and while I knew better than to fall asleep on him, maybe he had evolved in his thinking. I was spending zero waking hours at home by then and only slightly more than that at the shop, so I might not have had the full picture. Whatever his deeper truth, he had taken one last run at me, my head was still on its matchstick, and it was a relief to have it over with.

Farther along, the city staggered up again, made itself presentable. By presentable I mean the crowded-in jumble of giant curbs, brown brick facades, stairstep rooflines; clogged, circuit-board street traffic; throttling bus and semi engines; blunt echoes from dumpsters and waste cans; the numbing smack of street cellar doors. There were alternating smells of seeping sewage and breakfast counter grease; people who weren't so thoroughly dead on their feet as the few I'd looked-off a mile back.

Midtown, at the pedestrian mall, the farmers were setting up for their Saturday morning market. Straightaway I found my Zayde—my mother's father. He came every weekend to help one of the growers who used to sell to him when he owned his corner store. I tapped him on the shoulder and he wobbled into a half turn, locked onto me. Surprised and not surprised. He was past eighty, nothing could really throw him.

"Jeffrey!" he roared and swept me in with his huge, gentle strength. The man was a heroic hugger. He'd lean in and brush you with his scrub beard and thick, bark-like face, then nearly smother you with his incredible, old-world might. All you could do then was try to breathe and hold on.

Knowing better in those days than to ask questions, he turned and dug his hands into a crate of peaches. He found a soft one, passed it to me. No, rolled it in his hands first, placed it into mine, buried it there like a pitching coach does with a pitcher, then squeezed my upper arm and said, "Last of the year, try that. You can't beat that. They're sweet as sugar."

I asked if he'd mind my spending a few hours at his place, so he pulled out his big jailer's ring of keys to God-knows-what, probably all the coolers in the store he closed up a dozen years before, gave me directions I didn't need, told me how to unlock the door, jiggle the knob, which windows to open, what was in the fridge. As I broke away, I chomped into the peach. As good as advertised.

A couple of blocks along, I came upon Shelly, Lev. They were sweeping off the pavers in front of their by-then dying, decrepit shoe stores, which stood on opposite sides of the street, and trading polite but probably very sincere insults. There was no slipping past them, they placed me right away and would've had my entire ancestral map laid out in their heads: parents, grandparents, aunts and uncles, other familial ties through temple and the community. I knew the inside their stores, too, dragged there as a kid for new shoes and later as a helper on small rewiring jobs.

"*Yefei ben Avrom*," Shel said, taking hold of my sleeve, calling out to Lev. *My name, son of, his name.*

"Well, well," Lev muttered as he shuffled across to join us.

There was a faint shadow of rebuke in their eyes, though I had yet to open my mouth, and I can only assume now that it was the mere fact of me: my age, my hair, the lack of a recent shave, a general aura of impiety and shiftlessness. Also the fresh gash in my jeans, the road rash on my cheek …

"Such excellent service," Shel exclaimed, raising his arms in mock wonderment. "Not ten minutes after I call for an electrician."

"And the future proprietor of the business, no less. How can you go wrong?" The two of them still speaking only to each other. But then, Shel:

"Shouldn't you be off to university by now, young man?"

They leaned in together and stared. Unified in umbrage at any dishonor I might bring to my father and his father before him. An indigestive quality began to erupt in the silence between us.

"Aah! Disregard him," Lev gruffed, then gestured wildly in Shel's direction. "The world's biggest meddler. Always meddling."

"What meddling?"

"Always meddling. Always peddling."

"And you?"

"And me? Me? I have an establishment to run. A business. Enough of a business so that I don't need to concern myself with the business of others."

"Aah …"

"Aah …"

I followed Shel into his store. A ladder was set up in the dingy, narrow corridor that led from the display area to the back room, and boxes were stacked against the walls there from floor to ceiling. Shel flipped up his palms, tilted toward me, uttered in some low, grave tone that had the effect of ghosting the words in the air, "Shoeboxes: they're never just about the shoes, are they?"

Overhead, a single, naked tube blinked, buzzed. I kept my eyes only on that. Shel shrugged, ducked into the back, returned with a flashlight and screwdriver. I climbed the ladder and quickly took apart the fixture.

"You have a bad ballast here, Mr. Minchnik."

"This I divined on my own. It's the fixing of the thing that challenges. The restoration of light. It's a spiritual business you're in, eh, Jeffrey? Wasn't the plan for you to seek higher learning and then to return to it?"

"Unless you have a spare, Mr.—"

"Yes, yes. There is a box in storage with curious markings. A gift from the esteemed Elizando, who left without it on the occasion of his last service call. I have also a voltmeter and line crimper from that same visit. You are free to reclaim them."

Shel talked while I worked until I heard the words, or rather unscrambled the words several seconds after they were spoken, "Your mother's toes, they're the most delicate confections."

I stopped and stared down. Stared down at the top of his head. He blathered on. I rolled the screwdriver in my hand, considered staking it through his skull. Only Lev would know, and it's possible he wouldn't turn me in.

In those seconds, aloft in the dark, amid a swirl of dust, and in a sane but patently juvenile leap of logic that I can now only approximate, I arrived at the realization: this was the last act I would perform for the family business;

the business I was reared in, had become inured to, had not seriously conceived of a life apart from despite vague notions of escape that schooled through my head for months, years; the business, the birthright, I was told and had forever taken as an article of faith would be mine and my fate. If I were to make it out alive, it stood to reason, it would be with blood on my hands.

"So, it's settled then. You shall take my grandniece on a date!" said Shel, looking up, extending his hand, oblivious to the murder in my heart. *The screwdriver is a broom, the boxes are a fence, the bus runs right down this street. But the face, it's all wrong …*

Later, when I made it to Zayde's, I stretched out on the sofa and fell asleep gazing at a picture of my grandmother. As a kid I used to lie on that sofa, and she'd scratch my back with her thick, mutt-like nails and tell me how terrific I was. Two years had passed since she died. I doubted I'd ever get over it.

I felt a tap on my head, opened my eyes. Zayde's grinning, grizzly face. I had the sense he was stationed there awhile.

"I'm driving over to Charlie's for a trim. How about coming along? Let Charlie work on you?" Charlie's, the place he would drag me to when I was a shrimp. Even then an old-time, *old-timers'* barbershop.

"I don't think so, Zayde," I said, smiling sleepily at the thought.

"No? Then the next time I catch you napping here, I'll do it myself," he growled and gave me a rough, fork-fingered tousle.

"How did you make out at the market today?"

"How do I ever make out? The ladies come, I sell them the beans. That's how I made out."

I sat up and he grabbed both my ears, then came in with a loud, bristly smooch to the forehead.

"There's a sandwich for you on the kitchen table."

"Thanks."

"And some root beer in the icebox."

"Thanks."

"I'll see you later, then?"

"Probably not."

He gave me a hug before he left, another big, brawling hug, and I watched from the steps as he hobbled toward his car. He moved with his legs splayed wide, cane out even farther, searching for whatever stability he could find. He braced himself inside his old Plymouth wagon and crawled off. The rain still hadn't come but the sky was full of threat.

Guessing where my brother, Daniel, might be, I rang the house of one of his bandmates, then had to wait several minutes before he came on the line. Drums and guitars thrashed away in the background. I told him I needed a change of clothes.

"You still coming to see us play tonight?" he asked.

"I forgot all about that. I'm working."

"Come after."

"How late will you be there?"

"It's kind of loose."

"Are you gonna play that tonight?"

"Play what?"

"What I'm hearing. That's an A's song, isn't it?"

"I want to. Franny hates it, though. He can't work out the changes."

"I'd forget about the A's," I said: first, because The A's were too good, too revered across the entire tri-state area at that exact fraction in time—he would have known I meant that by the comment; and second, because, along the same basic lines, trying to knock him down every once in a while was something I did.

"Yeah, I hear you, J," he sent back, blowing right past the taunt, which was how he usually handled it.

"Anyway, come over around three. You can give me a lift to work."

Restless more than I was hungry, I wandered into the kitchen and found a wad of fried Minute Steak, along with an ooze of cheese from a can, pressed inside a toasted freezer-bagel. Arrayed around it on the table were ketchup, mayo, mustard, cream cheese, pickles, peppers, onions, chips. Basically, everything in the house that might relate to either a bagel or a cheese steak, much of it kept there strictly for Daniel and me. I hesitated a moment, took it all in, and I can still feel the arrow in my chest: the cheese steak, a venerated offering in that area, yet a desecration Zayde would have never parted his lips for. And there I was, sacked out in his living room, so he tried to get one together. Eventually I put the extras away and wolfed down a pickle—it was enormous—along with the chips. Just as I finished, the phone rang. I came close to answering and then guessed that it was, or rather understood that it could be, my mother. I let it ring that time and again a half hour later.

Just past 3:30, Daniel and Franny rumbled up in Franny's flame-painted, pogoed-up Chevelle.

"Where've you been?"

"We stopped at the Charcoal Pit. Franny wanted a malt."

"Did you at least get me one?"

"No, damn. We should've though."

"Fuck! Let's go. I'll change in the car. I'm already late."

The bagel was in my hand—I didn't want Zayde finding it in the trash—so I winged it in toward Franny, jumped into the back, and we tore off. I always felt stupid riding in Franny's car, and shunned it as a rule, though I had noticed the attention it caught from girls. It was a reminder that I had almost everything wrong, and Daniel and Franny had almost everything right: play in a band, cruise around in souped-up cars, get shitty grades, and somehow friends and girls are stuck on you at all times. I got slightly less shitty grades but not to the point that it even came close to making up for not getting laid. And not to the point, I should probably add, that it qualified me for anywhere except the state university, and only then on some sort of probationary deal—which, by that time, I had let pass anyway.

I wriggled into my department store job clothes while we roared along. Franny, I observed, was eyeballing the sandwich as he drove, turning it over in his free hand, appraising it in his mindless way.

"Remember that song from *Wally Gator*? We should play that tonight," Daniel said, looking hopefully at Franny.

"You're high, dude."

"No. We could work out a totally balls version of that. It'll kill."

A couple of rain splats hit the windshield, then Franny said, distractedly—still studying the sandwich, holding it up to the light—"I'm hungry. Let's stop at Jack in the Box."

"After you drop me off, Franny," I snapped. "And watch the road, will you?"

"When are you leaving town, boss? I thought you were clearing out months ago."

"We need another song, anyway," Daniel ran on, at which point Franny cradled the bagel in his palm, spooled it in, and obliterated it in two lunging bites. It traveled down his throat in a thick clod, like he just swallowed a frog.

"Man, that was all right," he belched. "Whatever the hell it was."

As we spun into the mall parking lot, I stuffed my boots and jeans into the sack Daniel had used for my store clothes, then leapt out while the car was still shuddering to a stop.

"Check us out tonight, Jeff," Daniel said as I straight-lined it for the store. My brother was that way with me, he wanted my approval—he was casual about it, but he did—and I hardly gave it to him. It was one of the few things in my life I felt I could control.

Racing in I passed Myers, and he shot me a hateful look. More hateful than usual, if that were somehow possible. My days were numbered there, I knew it.

Straight off I found Kim out in the aisles, and she told me that Reagor, another stock clerk, needed help in back. I tracked him down, and we spent a couple of hours stacking, unstacking, uncrating, moving things around, staging displays for the floor. It was all right hanging out with Reagor, even if I was fine always leaving it at the door. We horsed around a lot together. The work, too, helped me to relax.

Later, Kim circled around, and the three of us ducked beneath a catwalk and lit up. That girl, she always had some on her. It must have been a kick for her to get high with us, she being the supervisor, the one who should've been setting an example. In truth, she was twenty-one, only three years older. She wasn't pretty, but she had the appeal that average girls have who are willing to be pals with you. Her hair was stringy and cascaded down the sides of her head in sharp, shiny creases she never bothered to iron out. Her eyes were big and noncommittal and always floating away a little. And she was skinnier as a girl than I was as a guy, which is saying something.

After Reagor and I had things caught up, we put off searching for Kim or Myers to ask what they needed next. There was a locker we kept stocked with munchies from incoming loads, so we raided that, then we began racing the pallet jacks around. These jacks, they were solid iron and had wide, flat forks and an articulating post-handle you could use as a kind of front-end rudder. The idea was to stand on the forks, push off, and eventually get some speed going. All you had to do then was aim and hold on. They cornered amazingly well and would never tip, they were so damn heavy.

So, there we were, shooting between rack rows, having a blast, and still being faintly stoned wasn't hurting at all, when somehow the impossible happened: I lost control and plowed into several stacked, cut-away flats of Rose Milk. Reagor stood there laughing, doubled over, but I was shaken up. I had smacked my head on a shelf beam. Bottles of lotion lay everywhere, and several of them had burst open. It was a stinky, slimy mess, and I lay there and moaned and held my head.

"You idiot! You fuck-up! You complete and utter fuck-up!" cried Reagor, his voice coming at me from fifty different directions, colliding, echoing, overlapping … *Reagor, of all people, calling me an idiot.* It's crazy what you'll hold onto while you're falling away, falling under: the most twig-like hope; the most absurd rage. *Reagor,* I told myself then, with whatever reasoning was still available to me, *I'll strangle you for this.*

A minute later—some minutes later, I'm not sure—I heard Myers shout, "Get out! Get out of here. You're fired, Alexander. And Reagor, your ass is in trouble too."

"Fuck you," I rallied to say.

"Get out of here," he yelled again.

"You get out of here."

"I'll call goddamn security."

"They hate you, dickhead."

Eventually Kim stepped in, helped me to my feet, helped me get cleaned off and into the jeans and work shirt I'd worn earlier and was lucky enough to have with me. Steering me outside, away from Myers, away from Reagor, who by then I swore I was ready to get after—though almost certainly I wasn't, meaning she saved me from an even greater comedown—and picking up on the matter of my having no place to go, no way to get anywhere, Kim handed me a key, said I should hang out at her apartment, told me to rest there awhile and that maybe we'd do something later. It seemed impossibly kind, considering what I looked and smelled like at that moment.

Left on my own, my head screaming, I dropped to the curb and tried to gather myself. The rain had come and gone, but I wasn't even aware of that until I realized my ass was getting wet. I staggered off into the twilight, tugging at the seat of my pants.

Kim lived close enough to the mall, but between the mall and her place was the track, and without really thinking about it I climbed off the road shoulder and aimed for a side gate. What with the two jobs and lack of steady access to a car, I hadn't played the horses in weeks. Mounting the stairs to the grandstand, I heard the announcer call post-time for the fifth race. I made straight for a window—as straight as I could (holding a hand over one eye seemed to help)—picked a number, and got a bet down just in time.

"What happened to your face?" I heard a second before the starter's bell rang.

I turned and saw Mike, million-year-old Mike, stooped next to me, swiveled up at me. He was maybe four, four-and-a-half feet tall. Too small for his hat. Too small for his uniform. Too small for his sidearm, the holster and sidearm they issued to all the security guards there. The holster drooped down his hip like a slab of liver.

"I haven't had the greatest day," I said over the crowd, trying to hold steady while the words, the internal vibration of them, rattled through the loose gravel in my skull.

"Tell me about it! If it wasn't for bad days, I'd have no days at all," Mike blared, immediately launching into his Rodney Dangerfield routine, talking to me and everyone around us. Mike just had to be everybody's friend, all the time.

My horse broke last and appeared as though it would pretty much stay there the entire race. I didn't mind; in fact, I was kind of relieved. All the other horses were packed in tight, and I didn't want him to wade in there and get bounced around. I thought of my long walk across town that morning, how it was enough sometimes to just get out there and go. To stretch out a bit.

At some point during the race, I noticed my boots were flopped open, recalled pushing Kim away when she tried to lace them up for me in the store. I knelt to take care of this and, as I did, found myself inches away from Mike's holster. Measured from my nose, six inches. The curved heel of the revolver stuck out from its leather sock like a Labrador's snout; pointed straight ahead; pretended not to notice me; laughably, preposterously, denied the significance of it being there at that precise moment.

While everyone around us cheered, pumped their fists, urged on their bets, while Mike rocked from side to side in his orthopedics, I flicked the snap on his holster, lifted out the gun, and slipped it into my jeans. The beltline of my jeans, against the small of my back, where my shirttail would cover it best. I could feel the groove between the grip and chamber triangled at the base of my spine.

After the race ended, after Mike had finished with the backslaps and shouts of "Go on, go on, go get your money ya lucky SOBs," I said, in as dead level a voice as I could manage, and with as null an expression to match, and either out of brashness or stupidity or what may have even been an unconscious desire to be immediately found out, because an hour could have gone by before Mike caught on to the missing counterbalance to his limp—I said, "Hey, Mike, where's your gun?"

"My … my gun? My gun! Dammit! Goddammit, not again! Oh, Christ! Good goddamn Christ … Where the hell? … Did you see? … Oh God. I gotta go. I gotta go, kid."

"Mike! Mike! Who do you have in the sixth?" I called out as he skittered away, regretting instantly that I hadn't waited and ask first, as Mike occasionally had a line on these things, and if you laughed at his jokes and bought him a soft-serve every once in a while (or something else easy on his gums), and also if you were a kid (which, in his eyes, and as he had just stated, I still was), he'd be inclined to let you in on it. Provided, of course, you weren't one to squeal about it (you'd get one chance to prove that).

But then, "The sixth?" a stranger replied, lolling by in his railroad stripes. He stopped, leaned in, blew the words softly through a coned-up tip sheet: "Put it all on Filly Cheese. She loves the mud."

This was nearly a divine moment. A moment when everything crosses in the wind and becomes part of the same thing. When only a clear, sunlit expanse lies between the present and some new, more exalted reality. Yet to say nearly divine is to say not quite divine, in this case an almost paralyzing distinction. The fact is, what I knew and couldn't forget, what Mike had taught me, had jabbed into my navel the first time we met when he befriended me as did all the track rats who hung out at that sorry, sad, loser raceway instead of the million better places for kids to hang out, was that the horses with undignified names, they're sucker horses. They're there for first-timers, for women, for the astonishing number of people who'll bet good money on a bad joke. They're there to spike the pool, to lengthen the odds on the rest of the field. I knew this. I remembered this. Remembered it immediately. It was never not there in my head from the second the horse's name was lowly megaphoned into my face, even as I reveled in the wonder of it all. And yet, and yet … in the end, how could I—how could anyone—have passed? I obeyed the confiding voice, followed the lighted path. It wasn't so much a risk, I must in some sense have understood, as it was a risk not to. I counted out what remained in my wallet, seventeen dollars in all, and plunked down fifteen of it to win. Alas, the odds were long but not that long, the horse was indeed a mudder, so when it sloshed away from the field I felt redeemed but realized also that my circumstances were not very much changed. It did make my head feel better though. The slightest bit better.

At Claims I hung back, hung back, waited more or less for the lines to disappear. I had slid the gun around to the notch in my pelvis. My hands were in my pockets, and I began stroking the barrel through the nubby cloth—in the same manner, it occurs to me now, that I was constantly doing at that age with my own standard issue shooter. In fact, at the time, they were kind of knocking against each other. It was a strange feeling: one not so much of arousal as of affinity; reunification.

Eventually I moved in, pushed my ticket under the window with one hand, ran my palm over the gun handle with the other. There was a calculation going on, just outside my ears it seemed, where the knowledge that the glass was bulletproof, that the gates would lock down automatically, that guards were posted only a few yards away, that I had no idea how to operate this or any other real gun, held no sway … *This is your chance, you'll have your stake. You can finally get out of this dead-end town.* But as I eased the revolver over my hip, my skin tingling under the trace of the burnished metal, I heard a voice: a voice muted by the glass but one I recognized.

"Good lord! You look like you've been stamped on the head with a printing plate."

I opened my eyes. Rather, I made a concerted effort to focus my eyes, which had, in fact, been open but not quite seeing. I realized then that the claims clerk, the person standing opposite me and at whom I was about to aim a loaded—I presumed loaded—firearm, was someone I knew; someone I liked; loved, almost. My history teacher from the prior year. A decent all-around guy.

"Mr. Bloom," I breathed.

"What the blazes happened to you?"

"I … I hit my head."

"You hit your head. No kidding," he said, and then, after several seconds, the question still in his eyes but unrepeated, and in that deep, rolling tone that had always entranced me, "You might want to get an ice pack on that, Jeff. Sooner rather than later."

I laughed. I didn't mean to, but I did. A one-note laugh that fired out like a jet of compressed air. And while he wouldn't have known it, it was the forced release of that single pound of pressure that saved him. Or saved me. That allowed me to pull back. To stand stiff as he shrugged, slid the money through, and turned away. I picked up the bills and wandered off. Wandered off clutching them with the hand that didn't shoot, that didn't draw; that purloined a gun off a shrunken old rogue who had only ever shown me kindness; that had panged for a coworker's neck and never got hold of it; that steered a dolly into a pallet of pink bottles; that tightened around a screwdriver and failed to stab with it; that set the clip on a gas nozzle and then forgot about it; that rolled the joint that lit the fuse that set fire to most everything I had since touched; that, with one moment having passed to burn down whatever else remained and before another came along, covered one eye with a starched deck of inky green notes as I listed down the stairs and out again, out into the warm, wrung out, barely breathing night.

An hour or two passed before Kim showed up at her apartment.

"Jeff? Jeff?" I heard her call out in the dark. I wasn't asleep so much as adrift, stretched out on her futon, trying to contain, to trench around, the migrating pain in my head.

"What's that on your eyes, you goofball?" she asked and pulled on the corner of the dishtowel, causing the by-then not entirely frozen calzone to dive out and whomp to the floor.

"It was the only thing in your freezer," I said.

"Let me see …"

"Ouch!"

"It doesn't look so bad. It could be a lot worse."

"I'll pay you for that, Kim."

"For what? For that?"

"No joke, Kim. I'm flush."

"I won't even respond to that," she said, then shoveled up the calzone and dropped it in the trash.

She had brought home the last of the soft pretzels from the store carousel, so we daubed them with mustard—mustard being one of the few things she kept in her refrigerator—and downed them with a couple of beers—beers being another. I asked her if she remembered Mr. Bloom, the history teacher, from her high school days—she did—and informed her that he was moonlighting at the track. "He was a really, really nice guy," she said thoughtfully, which at first I was gratified to hear and then felt a little betrayed by.

Later I mentioned Daniel's band had a gig at a party that night. For some reason Kim latched on to the idea, which surprised me, as everyone there was bound to be younger than she was. Still, I couldn't land on an excuse for not going, other than the welt on my forehead and its accompanying ache, which she dismissed out of hand, so after a while we did make our way there. Mike's gun was still tucked in my jeans, and I was of a mind to ditch it on the drive over, but there was no practical way for that to happen. Not with Kim sitting beside me.

We heard the guitars ripping before she even turned off the car. Following the noise, we found the band set up inside a dim, low-ceilinged rec room. A handful of kids dotted the far wall, others drifted throughout the house. Daniel sang better than I would have guessed, and Franny and the guys kept time well enough. Overall I was impressed, though hardly anyone was paying attention. It was odd seeing my little brother that way, strutting around like he was the center of the world. He totally ignored me when we walked in, as if he were too uplifted by the music. Maybe he was. Still, I caught a sliver of an eye checking out Kim for an instant, which means he definitely knew I was there.

The band took a break after that song, so I introduced Kim around, all the while swatting away comments about my head, my clothes, Kim, even though she stood right next to me. At one point Daniel pulled me aside and said, "Whatever it was with Cale, bro. That sort of made the news back at the house."

"I wasn't sure that actually happened."

"It happened."

I glanced back for a second and saw Franny chatting up Kim. He had a way of slouching backward when he talked to a girl so that his dick was the closest thing to her. Kim's arms were crossed, her legs soldered together, and she stood perfectly straight, giving her an elongated, sculptured aspect. Her eyes sailed away, sailed around the room.

"Mom wants to know what's going on," Daniel continued.

"That's a laugh."

"You know what I mean."

"That's a complete fucking laugh."

"You know, though. She wants you home tonight. She wants things blown over."

"I mean, that's just completely, totally, fucking amazing," I said, then brushed past him, seeing the bathroom free up.

As soon as I was inside, I lurched into a dry heave, then another, and another, before backing out and careening down the hallway toward the front door, away from the economy-sized jug of Rose Milk assaulting me from the ledge of the vanity. Stumbling from the house, splitting with rage, the entire morning-till-night accumulation about to burst from inside me, unable to keep my arms from swinging, my feet from kicking a wall, a tree, a mailbox—*another mailbox*, and perhaps it was a flinching memory of that rifle and the CAT hat behind it that made me think twice, or just think—I banked over to Franny's Chevelle, jumped onto the front bumper, unzipped, and aimed for the outrageously huge air dam welded to its hood. Only the initial blast made it into the mouth of the dam, the rest streaming out toward the gullies just inside the front fins. This is the progression, I must somehow have believed: that last leap toward higher ground where nothing more ridiculous than what had already happened could happen; the kind of end-all moment where Kong clings to a building, bellows in fury, takes the only revenge available to him before a death fall. But then I heard a flat, familiar voice say, "I'll just stand here until you're finished," and as I twisted to locate her, the revolver dropped from my waist, banged off the grille, and twirled to the ground.

"Nice," she said. "Really. That's nice. That's excellent."

"Kim—"

"No. Really. That's excellent. I'm hanging out with a guy who has a gun with him and is going to use it for … exactly what?"

"I'm not—"

"I mean, how excellent? How excellent is that?"

"I'm not using it for anything, Kim. It's not even my gun."

"I mean, God, Jeffrey! Just God!"

She stared straight at me. Her eyes weren't adrift. They weren't noncommittal. There was a storm drain in the street a few yards away, so I gave the gun a shove with my foot, watched it skip over the pavement, rattle between the grates, and clank down below. Kim stomped to her car and got in, but she waited there, so after a while I walked over and slid in next to her. As I did, she swung around, swung her whole collection of shoelace limbs on top of me. She glommed her mouth to mine, augured her tongue through, slithered her hands between and around, over and under. It was like being mauled by a warm, smoky-smelling squid. After a minute, probably not even a minute, we began to squirm into position, pull at each other's clothes, feel for buttons and zippers, the situation having been transformed into an immediate crisis. But there was nothing at all to be done. I exploded in my jeans before she could even pry it out.

The following morning, Daniel picked me up at Kim's place and drove me to the Front Street terminal. He had filled a duffle with my things, the few I thought I'd need. We kept the windows open along the way, let the wind roar, the city blur past. It saved us from having to talk or to feel as though we should.

I tried not to have pangs for Kim, to tamp down anything at all like that. She was really patient with me during the night, really sweet, more than I had any reason to expect. But dwelling on it wasn't going to help me, to steel me up. I knew that.

Daniel stepped out with me at the station and tagged along as far as the concourse. I couldn't tell what was going through his mind, but I gave him a quick hug and told him everything'll be fine. He said, "Yeah, I know," and then added, "Look, we got paid last night, so this is yours," and lifted a handful of bills from his pocket. There were more than a few dollars there, I could see. Enough for him to have thought twice about it.

"All right," I said, and not because I couldn't afford to refuse, though that was certainly the case. But it was just one of those things … I knew instinctively it would connect us, give him a stake in whether I made it or not. Like at the track, if you gave your money straight to the horse and the horse understood.

"You guys sounded pretty good last night," I offered. "At least that song I heard."

"Thanks," he said and gave me a sleepy but happy, completely unrueful smile. "Mind if I join up with you in a couple years?"

I wasn't able to answer him at first and then saw that I didn't have to. He was just giving me one last boost.

After buying a ticket, one way to San Francisco, a hundred and fifty stops along the way—the destination I have no memory of deciding upon, though it's a laugh to imagine having landed anywhere else—and with time to kill, I set off through the vacant streets near the terminal. Not very far along, I spotted a lone soul in a newsboy cap letting himself into a storefront and, coming close, realized I'd lucked upon Charlie's, the barbershop, and that the old guy must be Charlie himself. I pressed to the glass and peered around, but nothing about the place seemed familiar. It had been way too long.

I wondered what he was doing there on a Sunday, then guessed that he lived above. Still, I had this notion, this sense of something extra, something promising that, if not entirely like that moment at the raceway, was elevated in its own right. So I rapped on the glass and motioned toward the door and, when he opened it, asked if he was free just then. He shrugged and answered, "Sure, sure, why not?" gazing at me without disdain but also without recognition. That was okay. I wasn't there to talk or to go back in time.

As I ducked inside, Charlie, or the guy who, in this one particular light, lives on in my mind as Charlie, snapped out an apron and gestured toward the lone, ancient pump chair situated in the middle of the floor. I gave him the signal and he pretty much mowed everything off. It felt good, it felt lasting and memorable, the cool, firm rake of the shears across my head.

CASUAL AGENT ON A SAFE ISLAND

It came as a deprivation in that moment not to breathe in flesh and hair and scent. I leaned against the archway, tried to quiet my senses. I fell immediately under the conviction I belonged on the other side of the door, but that didn't come from my head.

Most of the buildings on the block stood obscured in the murk of the hour, though dashes of light lined the street-level window of the one I had just exited. Devi had mentioned that a dealer lived there, said he conducted business throughout the night—activity she would be aware of, as her apartment lay directly above. I considered checking out the situation. I wasn't in the market and had mostly left that chapter behind. But she spoke with a glimmer of something other than indifference about the guy, so there was more to find out if we were to continue seeing one another.

As I walked to the car, I felt the need to reshape my mouth with my tongue, my lips gone to mush from all the kissing. And inside I was all heat, from my bones to my skin, the buildup from nearly an entire evening of physical torment. I even broke into a jog for several steps, as if it were possible to outrun, then pulled up short. One of the lobby ghosts who hung out at the brokerage would lecture us on spontaneous combustion, and he told us one day, "If you feel it coming on, stand on your head. It reverses the valence of the electrons and your cells can't ignite." Having taken in enough by then of all that San Francisco had to offer, it brought me to the realization: not becoming like that guy, and the countless others of his type there, was a commitment I would continually have to make.

Not ready for the night to end, I drove west through the park and headed to the one place I felt sure of being welcome at 2:00 a.m. The trees, in the dark, joined to a fluttering curtain along either side of Kennedy Drive, and a faint sense of affliction as to what lurked behind began to drift through me. I had only spent a single night outside, my fourth in town, and only half of it in the park. Yet it marked a certain through-the-trapdoor culmination. For years I went out of my way to avoid being reminded of it. That I no longer bothered amounted to a reckoning of a kind, an acceptance that more than just time had passed. I had landed in a decent apartment, finally; drove a car I half owned; occasionally had a little money; could have even claimed a degree if State hadn't denied certain credits brought over from City College. The prospect of ever sinking that low again had become easier to ignore.

As I cut out to the upper avenues, a patrol car appeared and began to shadow me. My first thought was to try for George's place while still having a choice in the matter, that he would come down and work things out with the guy. I couldn't attend traffic school for another nine months and seriously did not want to pay the fine for fifteen over, about what I was going. Yet it occurred to me in the duration of the same held breath that a real cop would never have anything to do with a fake cop, and

George was, by his own admission, a fake cop. Part of the city's Environmental Brigade. He was a sworn officer of the law and even wore blues, but the only ticket he might have saved me from would have been for not keeping my recycling in order.

At last the strobe came on, but as I eased to the curb the cruiser sped up and blew past me. I sat there a minute, first to make sure it wouldn't double back, then to absorb my good luck. I heard sirens converge from multiple directions and then fade, and maybe I did or maybe I didn't wonder about the intersecting event. Relief over a situation like that can be a fairly blunt feeling.

I left the car there, not at all assured of finding a closer spot, and walked the last several blocks to the flat George shared with his sister Regina and her toddler. Instead of buzzing me in, he radioed, "Stay there, we'll go for a walk," then skipped down the stairs a minute later wearing his familiar surplus-store sailor's coat and skinny-leg jeans. An unstable, fermented air drafted along with him.

"I can get you something warmer than that," he said, taking note of my turtleneck-only status.

"No," I told him, "I'm looking forward to cooling off," which won a questioning look from him, though not an actual question.

It was, to be clear, frigid outside, as it almost always is in the Outer Richmond at night regardless of the time of year. The mist fell in such high relief you could see the softest wind thread through it, and the view in all directions disappeared in the vapor beyond a few short blocks. Generally the neighborhood had a quiet, anonymous feel to it and was thought to be safe, though a couple of notorious gay-beatings had unfolded there in prior months. George, for whom this wasn't an abstract concern, remarked at the time, "Here's what I don't understand. Those guys were already gay. The hierarchy didn't need to be reinforced."

I considered occasionally in those days, and quite possibly at that moment, how in the schoolyards of my youth there had often been gays, and fags and queers, and how I suffered my turns as each of them. Such were the cruelties among boys in times past, the language of tolerance having not yet found us. And perhaps this acclimated me in a way to the city I'd later reside in, however unimagined such a place may have been. Once there, it was far from lost on me, and not without corroboration, that I might be cuter to guys than I ever was to girls—a reminder of which came daily at my workplace, as much as I sought to shrink from it.

"Now I remember. The date with the girl from India, that was tonight," George said as we climbed the hill up Cabrillo Street. George lived twenty blocks from the ocean, and we had automatically set off in that direction. Even with the chill, the steep ascent had us both panting within the first minute.

"She is East Indian. She grew up in Fiji, though."

"Tonight, right?"

"I just came from her place."

"How did it go?"

I didn't have a ready answer. In one respect it should have been obvious, yet I couldn't quite pull it together. What arrived for me in the moment that followed took the form of a kind of signal graph: a perspective of Devi, or my involvement with Devi, as no more than the latest spike in the essentially flat line of possibility extending forward from the breakup with Gail nearly two years before.

There had been a few others: the flameout with the sister of the Israeli guy who had sold me the car; the completely botched situation with Tula from my previous job, which cost me a friendship not only with her—I never asked for more than that from Tula—but a half-dozen other people I enjoyed hanging out with; and then, of course, the lone and intensely disappointing, for her, and debasing, for me, experience with Stephanie.

Stephanie, the gem among them all. The one I had no business even trying for. Sunny, intelligent, attractive in a lax, unintentional way that could trail a guy along, she had spent her entire life in the city and had that unmistakably native, informed perspective as proof of it. She was in her last year of residency in oral surgery at UCSF, the clinic where I'd had a gum graft because it was so much cheaper. On my final checkup I landed the date. This placed me well outside my range, and I knew better than to count on staying there. The whole progression with Gail had taught me that. Still, it's a challenge, a big challenge at the start of any new romantic situation, to keep the clamps on all inklings of hope, and a week remained before the first non-doctor-patient appointment in which to contend with visions of improbable, upbeat outcomes.

She came around in her parents' old Saab. I didn't yet have the Mustang. I had never been in a Saab and it struck me as an odd appliance: the sledding roofline, the floor-anchored ignition, the viewfinder effect inside the cabin. As we drove away, it rocked on its axis like an arcade pony, then stormed ahead in a fit of uncoordinated activity. I said, "Stephanie, it's as if it evolved in parallel with cars from all other parts of the world. Just like with people. It's more or less the same but also entirely distinctive."

And then I thought, *For an opening, for a first improvised thought, that wasn't bad. That was okay. Say something else.* I began to line up another winner; began, encouraged as I was by hitting a conversational note barely recognizable as my own, to think, *This might work out. I might do all right tonight.* That alone should have stopped me; should have sent me out of the car and on my way home. Because, the truth is, whenever I look back on my worst moments—and I know this isn't only me—the most indelible among them are those where I felt right on top of things beforehand.

"Jeff," she said and turned to face me—we were stopped at a light—"I'm sorry, I have to apologize if I seem upset"— she didn't, or hardly at all; it was as if she was about to relate a story she had heard or read about which saddened her in a remote, impersonal way. I thought that, and I also thought, taking in certain already favorite aspects of her, the loose, flyaway hair, the pale freckles colonized upon her cheeks and forehead, the sincere, devoted-to-the-present gaze, *You are so incredibly beautiful.* In fact, I could have made that my next comment, my next spot-on observation. It wouldn't have been very smooth, but it would have been honest, and I'll bet Stephanie would have appreciated it. But then she continued, "I found out for sure a couple of days ago that I have herpes simplex, and it's really been a downer for me."

It's not clear what happened next. I may have hopped away an inch. There might have been—almost assuredly was—an imprint of astonishment on my face belonging exclusively to that moment. All I can relate with certainty is what for an instant I saw, envisioned: an image of Stephanie looming over me, inches from my face, then up to her elbows inside my mouth with a melon knife.

Beyond that came clairvoyance, enlightenment, an open space where the already received knowledge of how one actually contracts herpes could emerge, affirm I remained free and clear up to that moment, safe, then reassemble to the belief that all Stephanie had done, in the course of being Stephanie, was to give me a heads-up, tell me she took me seriously enough to offer the disclaimer. Still, the journey had to be made. And she saw it. She saw the transition. It registered entirely and unmistakably.

"I'm sorry," I threw out there. "That must have been difficult. You found out for sure a couple of days ago, how? Wait, you don't have to answer that. Are you all right? Would you like me to drive?"

She bit down as long as she apparently could, then said, "No. No, Jeff, it's fine. I'm fine. Really, it's perfectly safe to drive with herpes."

"That's not what I meant."

"What did you mean?"

"I just … I just meant … I have no idea what I meant."

"This can't be happening," she said, twisting away, her voice trailing after her. I held off for what seemed a definitive interval, on the possibility that she might be right—that it wasn't actually happening.

"It's green," I told her.

"What?"

"The light. It's green. Or it was, a second ago."

"Oh, sorry. That's funny, isn't it? I guess I should have taken your offer seriously."

"Stephanie …"

"Well, okay," she said. "But we're still on a date, aren't we? Even if it started five minutes ago, and already there's a communicable disease involved. We can still have the evening out, I think," and the rebuke came less in her words than in her effort to disarm them.

"Sure, we can do that," I played along, realizing that was all she expected of me. I had tumbled all the way back to the flat line. Any attempt at that moment to climb up off it wouldn't have mattered. Later, at the end of the evening, after a bleak though not necessarily awkward time—awkward would have implied a certain possibility, a diminished yet not altogether forgone sense of hope—I did try to kiss her, if not exactly in the vicinity of her lips. A last shot to show I knew things; to claw back a little dignity, an element of masculine advantage. But she wouldn't let me connect and sent over a flat, discerning smile that said, in effect, "You're kidding, right?" I would see her again, her and the Saab, though not for another year and entirely by accident. Despite everything, I would be glad I did.

"There was just an election in Fiji," George said after we had traveled several blocks in silence through the marine air. The clearance to the cloud cover had begun to lift a little as we dropped down toward the beach. The low, heavy static of the sea blew steadily up toward us. "The Indians won. Or some sort of unity coalition. Did she mention it?"

"We never got around to politics. She said a lot of East Indians live there."

"Nearly half the population. They've never had control of national government. It's a significant story, a lot could change. Land tenure, residency rights, parliamentary rules—"

"You just happen to be up on all this."

"My father was stationed there for two years. We lived with him for maybe half of that."

"I thought that was the Philippines."

"The Philippines, Fiji, New Hebrides … though it's not called that anymore."

George was half Filipino—British national father, employed for decades in the U.K. diplomatic corps, and Manila born-and-raised mother—so I suppose I had focused on that. Or perhaps he hadn't mentioned the rest. George would let things out about himself when asked but never volunteered much.

"How old were you?"

"A kid. I don't remember a lot. But we did call it home for a while, so when I read or hear something about it, I'll pay attention."

"She left four years ago, when she turned sixteen. She's only twenty, that was one of the surprises of the evening."

"One of?"

"Her family is traditional. In at least one important respect. They had arranged a marriage for her—some guy from India she met as a child and can hardly remember. So when the time came, she bolted. They have no idea where she is. She says they'll kidnap her if they find her."

"And force her to go back? How would they accomplish that?"

"I didn't ask. It's my new policy. Don't react right away to shocking disclosures."

"You may want to allow for the occasional exception," he said after allowing the reference to sink in. "Say, when your date can be abducted at any moment."

"I didn't perceive an imminent threat," I replied, which was both true and in keeping with the tenor of his advice. "Besides, at the time, there were other things I was trying to sort out. Like I think she's seeing the guy who lives in the apartment below hers. Who happens to be a dealer.

And she doesn't exactly hold back on first dates. Well, she does and she doesn't."

"Only one of those sounds like any kind of problem in particular."

"You don't understand. She was—voracious. Just incredibly physical, almost from the start. And then she kept me there. Right on the verge. For hours."

"'Verge' needs to be accompanied by a predicate, unless you've already made it clear—"

"That wasn't clear? I'm pretty sure it was clear, George. Unless you're implying something completely original was about to happen."

"So, you're telling me you didn't talk politics …"

We both laughed, and for some stumbling number of seconds I became trapped in the almost visible swarm of George's breath. He favored pure malt spirits, and his need in recent months had become extreme, even in a place notorious for its inspired drunks. And George *was* inspired. His go-nowhere job with the city—the only steady job I'd known him to have, dating to my first hour in town when he offered me a lift from the Greyhound station to the Fort Mason hostel in his SFPD-issued, battery-powered three-wheeler—was always secondary. He was a playwright, an accomplished one. The Asian American Theater Company had staged his work, a highly reputable troupe then and now. And he would write and direct for other ensembles as well. Yet nothing had broken his way in a while, and finding him as I had that early morning—half-wrecked, jittery, in need of getting out—that was the pattern. He wouldn't have slept. His eyes would appear flat, washed over, drowning inside themselves. And there was often a fractured, incomplete aspect to his entire being, as if the alcohol had sieved him through.

"You should bring her over next time," he said. "Maybe she'll be impressed by your having a friend who lived in Fiji."

"I'll do that. If I see her again."

"Honestly? If?"

"We left it open. No, we didn't even do that. Once we got back to her apartment, there wasn't a lot of talking. Practically none. Two hours later I was standing outside, watching her walk back upstairs. She has this hair. A waterfall of black hair."

"Let's go over this. Here she is … this young, alluring castaway. Entirely on her own. Cut off from her past, her home, her family, from this tradition-bound culture she's known all her life—"

"I don't know about all that. I only know about the arranged marriage. It may have been pretty liberal until then."

"All right. Assume it was. It still strikes very deep, doesn't it? The latent orphanhood. The replacement need. The desperation expressed in her wanting to throw herself at guys. How could you not want to save her?"

"Take advantage of her, you mean," I said, not trying to make a point exactly, just a little tired of the conversation.

He tilted back his head, let several seconds pass before answering: "Take advantage—that's bracing. Really. Self-awareness is an admirable though not entirely practical trait in arriving at a certain endpoint in these situations. My guess is it was you who held back tonight."

I brushed off the remark but couldn't dismiss it outright. Devi had encouraged me, I wasn't wrong about that.

She allowed me significant and immediate liberties. Yet she steered me away every time I tried to move things toward that universally desired result. Had I not tried hard enough?

A couple of blocks along, we arrived at the shore and immediately began to wish we hadn't. Several patrol cars were there, as were far more souls than we had counted on given the hour. We crossed the Great Highway and peered over the seawall. The beach ran side-to-side and down from there like the slope edge of a ruler. Flares were lit in a half-moon pattern by the waterline, and a quiet, unorganized crowd lingered nearby. At first, we speculated an injured seal had washed up and they were trying to keep people away. But a guy standing near us said no, it was a person, all torn up and bloated. He said he'd had a look before the police arrived and was extremely sorry he had.

Eventually one of the officers separated from the scene and began to trudge toward us. The fluoro stripes on his rain shell acquired in the middle distance a certain motile, exoskeletal effect. Reaching the top of the stairs, and without any discernible greeting, he and George fell into conversation. So real cops would talk to him, it turned out. I listened while they went over the possibilities: a surfer; a deckhand gone overboard while paying out a longline; a jumper, swept all the way out and around from the bridge; or, more plausibly, by their estimation and my own, someone who ignored all the signs and ventured too far out along the rocks by the Sutro Baths. That happened once a year, no matter what. "You should go write that kid up," the cop cracked to George at one point. "He's stinking up the whole beach." Hearing that it was a kid threw me a little. Evidently the body wasn't so far gone that they couldn't tell.

Behind us, the intermittent zoom of cars over damp pavement created a kind of echo to the sizzle of water over sand along the ocean's edge. Gulls blared overhead, but only occasionally would they dip down where you'd catch sight of them, batting around in the misty red light. I said a quiet thank you to the kid, the victim, whatever, realizing his arrival there had saved me from a ticket. I wasn't trying to be jokey, like the cop. It was the most personalized sentiment I had to offer, that's all.

I was freezing by this time, and the scene at the beach had drained away whatever enthusiasm the two of us had for keeping the night going. Otherwise we would have gone down near the water and smoked a bowl. Or George would have, and I would have tagged along.

"I found a body once," George said as we trekked back inland. "On the beach, like this one. Near Drake's Bay."

"I thought you were going to say, 'stuffed in a dumpster.'"

"I do keep expecting that."

"What did you do?"

"Nothing. It looked more like driftwood than bones. And it wasn't a complete set or even a perfectly matched one, necessarily."

"That sounds more like a relic than a body. You might have had something there. An old mariner. Maybe Drake himself."

"Hah! I don't think so. You do still need a Bay Area history lesson every once in a while, don't you?"

"Whoever it was, they did you the favor of getting cleaned up first … which is better, I think. You know, if it has to happen, and if there's a chance you'll be discovered, stay out there awhile. Let the process play out. It seems preferable."

George blew into his hands, strode backward for several steps. He said, "I've got one for you," and went on to lay out a scene as unsettling to remember as it has proved impossible to forget. Years before, he helped out with a production at some underground theatre in L.A. The central premise, allowing now for a certain conflation of memory and nightmare, was one of decomposition's relationship to the mourning process. An open coffin lay on stage for the duration of the performance with a body prop, or a series of body props inside it showing the advancing stages of rot and reduction. In the last act, a skeleton only. The bereaved heroine, having passed through the various stages of grief and recovery, now down to the most hardened, mineralized sense of, or perhaps connection to, her dead lover. A certain irreducible construct of pain and acceptance. "As metaphors go, not an especially nuanced one," George said. "But having the body there, that was novel. The writer even wanted to have a stench piped in."

"I'm not sorry I missed it" was the truest thing I could think of to say.

"Yeah, I guess you won out on that one," he replied, and we hiked up and over the remainder of the hill in silence. We were done with any discussion about what we had just seen.

Idling outside his flat, I took in again George's diminished frame, shattered complexion. His face was glossed with moisture, and in the near absence of light it flashed like a playing card extended between two fingers. He said in a speculative way, "I like the culture clash aspect. And the intrigue. There are possibilities there. Not one without the other, but together … plus the notion of her being this sort of enchantress. What does Devi mean?"

"I don't know. And enchantress, I wouldn't say that. Just a little … wanton, maybe."

"Not as evocative."

I could see where he was going with this and wasn't about to encourage him. These were early days with Devi, if they were anything at all, and I didn't need to have them workshopped. He let me off the hook, though, and said, "You can take my coat if you want," the sort of line he was always coming out with—a tendency that traced to my arrival from the east coast and all the help he had been to me then. And since. Good for me, overall. Though I had begun to suspect the roles might reverse one day.

"That's okay," I told him. "I'm not parked far. Besides, there's a nice, warm body waiting for me back at the apartment. Oh, wait. There's not. That was two years ago. She can't stand the sight of me now."

George delivered the smile I'd meant to receive, and I left him planted there on the stoop, steam jetting through his teeth. I wasn't seriously pining for Gail. On some level, she was still in my head, but after that much time you've either moved on or you really are in trouble. *Maybe he can write that story*, I thought and had a laugh over it: the long-lost cause somehow easier to offer up than the one that hasn't come to anything yet. And may never. *Hell, George is probably right, I blew it tonight. It was all lined up for me, and somehow I missed it. So much for desperation sharpening the senses.*

I drove slowly to my apartment, stayed off all the main boulevards. Getting a ticket then would have meant throwing a gift in the face of that sorry kid tumbled up on the beach. I didn't want to do that.

Rhys would assume a deliberately arch manner whenever any of us received a personal call at work, something he seemed uncannily able to discern. He took far too pressing an interest in our social lives, especially among those of us he favored, youth and unattachment being the qualifiers. He would corral us into all-night dance outings at I-Beam or Silhouettes, or to free-form gatherings at his Cow Hollow flat where he held sway of a kind unavailable to him elsewhere. And he openly encouraged and enjoyed the sexual tensions and relationship dramas that inevitably played out among us.

I tolerated this at the time so as to remain agreeable to Rhys. He had brought me over from the brokerage where he first hired me and thrown in an extra thousand a month, so it was worth the halfhearted effort—leaving aside those occasions when I received a call at the office from a friend and wished not to be harassed about it; have him sail past my desk hoping to catch a few words. Rhys did sail when he walked, a fair wind at his back devoted to him alone. Or so he would have us imagine.

"Jeff? Are you still there?" Devi had finally asked.

"Sorry. I'm here."

"Is something wrong?"

"No, nothing," I said, not wanting to start in on the whole Rhys story. It wouldn't have come out right.

"You're going to make me plead, aren't you?"

"Plead?"

"Because of Sig."

"I think you've misunderstood—"

"I wouldn't have called you if I hadn't ended it. If it wasn't completely over now."

"Devi, just so we're talking about the same thing: Sig—the guy downstairs?"

"Yes, the guy downstairs."

I became distracted by the homophone—was it Sig or *Cig*, purveyor of sundry intoxicants—and left alone for a moment Devi's impatience with me. Which I may have done anyway. Three months had passed since we'd seen one another and there had been no contact. No calls, no second date. Then suddenly she was on the line. I wasn't sure how to proceed.

"It's not the best time to talk," I said.

"I'm sorry. I shouldn't have bothered you. I wasn't honest with you last time, and it's unfair of me to expect—"

"Devi, listen. I knew you were with that guy. It wasn't any business of mine, so you don't need to apologize. I am glad you called, though."

"Are you? Because it's difficult to tell. And I'm not—*I'm not* with him anymore. Or anyone. Please say you believe me about that."

"Alright, I believe you," I said, then jumped to the end of the conversation by promising to see her that coming weekend.

"Oh, I believe you, I do," came Rhys's taunting refrain from over my shoulder. "And with such ardor in your voice, Jeffrey. Who wouldn't be swept away?"

"I was speaking with your boss. You work for me now."

"Jeffrey, Jeffrey …"

"Don't you have an office to run?" I said, still not turning around, yet careful not to sound too annoyed. I could kid him, but it wouldn't have benefitted me to threaten his sense of entitlement.

"Yes, I do. But it's rather hard with my children fraternizing away their days at our benevolent company's expense."

"Try not to think of us as children, Rhys. That would be a positive first step."

He ignored me.

"Jeffrey, a word to the wise … or, in this case, to the smitten: I would resort to 'I love you' well, well before saying 'I believe you.' It's a lower standard. A far more flexible construct to commit oneself to."

I let it drop there. Rhys wanted most of all to know the details, and prolonging the conversation would have only rewarded his prying. Still, I couldn't immediately shake off what he had said. Love was the lower standard? Perhaps the less credible, I thought. The less essential in the very long run.

I watched him circulate throughout the office. He moved from the waist down, only. Self-consciously erect. Gliding airily among the cubes, a balloon figure on a parade float.

Later that afternoon, Maurizio dropped by on a final roundup for his party on Saturday. It occurred to me to bring Devi—originally I hadn't planned to attend. Maurizio was a friend, but he had transferred to the bond desk, and his trader pals were sure to have been invited. I didn't care for those guys, they were all very cocky and tended to look down on anyone from the retail side. There was also a chance, a mid-level chance, of seeing Gail there. If Maurizio's recently exed girlfriend Jennifer were to come, then Gail might be with her, as she and Jen were close—something we were always careful to work around.

I had made the commitment to Devi, though, and saw an opportunity to impress her. Any party of Maurizio's would be a scene. It wasn't clear why Devi called or what she might be after, but I wasn't inclined to worry about it. Just hearing her voice, her breath, had triggered the sense, the reexperience in some slight, penetrating way, of the physicality of our first date, as well as the frustration with how it had finished, or been left unfinished. *If Gail does come*, I managed to remind myself, *I'll have to deal with any grief that causes Devi*, realizing she might take the appearance of an old girlfriend as payback for the Sig thing. But that could be handled. And later arrived this consideration: *Devi's such a raw, ravenesque beauty, and so young … Gail will laugh when she sees us together, but it might get to her. It would be nice if it did.*

"So, what do my darlings have planned for the weekend?" asked Rhys, speaking to us all while looking straight at me, a smile of … what—amusement? condescension? lament?—revealing more than I ever cared to know. The day had wound down, and several of us were gathered by the door. Moira, a new girl, usually a little sad and quiet, though thankfully not at that moment, missed the subtext and began chatting in earnest about the advocacy walk she was involved in and to which most of us had pitched in a few dollars. It was enough for me to evade the question and slip away. The thought arrived, as it always did, *I'll know Rhys has given up on me when he stops with all this.* We were years into it by then, but I'd have known. It would have been easy. Rhys barely acknowledged guys he felt offered no prospect.

———

I drove out to Cole Valley to fetch Devi before heading downtown. She was dressed in black, her hair swam down and around her slender neck, the flare of her shoulders. I noticed the stark rims of her eyes, the violet gloss on her lips and fingernails, a metal choker and bracelet—anything that pooled the light. She seemed perfectly her age, at first, but no, the thought of her being twenty had worked on my mind over the prior few months, she was just as she had been before, the accentuation of her features and a certain dauntlessness in her gaze extending the range within which she could roam.

She was willing from the start, but I had a different attitude this time. Perhaps not as grateful for my good fortune. I felt nothing lasting was at stake, nothing beyond what might be accomplished that evening. I liked Devi but had decided to set that aside. She might have still been with Sig, she might not, it wouldn't have mattered. She was the one who called, and while that only counted for so much, my role, at least in my own imagination, had become clearer.

With traffic, parking, and all the clinging and mauling, it took us an hour to make it to Maurizio's apartment, and I didn't necessarily want to go in by the time we had. My whole body tingled. We had engaged in exactly zero substantive conversation by that point.

Devi said, "We could skip this. You live close by, don't you?" though it came off as a tease, a promise for later, not something to take seriously. I would soon and for a long while after wonder about not having gone on to the next order of thought: that there were times when it paid to make the most of an insincere offer, and how important it was to be able to distinguish those times.

The first face, the first animate object we encountered after stepping through the door was the biggest prick of all from the bond desk. He pounced on Devi—immediately began hitting on her, unbothered by my having walked in alongside her. Devi didn't resist; seemed, in fact, enthralled inside the smarm that came off him. I stood there, atomized by the sudden detonation in circumstances. It was brazen, and I could have slugged the guy or absorbed the humiliation, there existed in that moment no middle strategy I could articulate for myself. Intuitively I knew I shouldn't overprotect—Devi would have hated that—but intuition, or, rather, better judgment as filtered through intuition, did not yet have the hold on me that a few additional life lessons would eventually provide, and it could have easily let go once again ... if not for the fact that Maurizio, and another guy I knew well, Eric, from Treasury—we'd all started with the company on the same day two years before—materialized in that instant in front of me.

"We've been waiting for you, Jeff. It's been another year and we decided we need to drink to that," Eric said by way of greeting. And then Maurizio: "It wasn't a particularly hard decision."

I gazed at them, registered their faces; after a few seconds, arrived roughly at this thought: *Okay, I'll have a conversation several feet away from my date while another guy chats her up. A confident person can do that. And Devi will appreciate it.*

Eric had gone on to say, "I hear you're headed to Marketing."

"Wrong," I told him, that first word being more of an exhale. "I interviewed, got shot down. You know Jim Lorrie?"

"I know who he is. Pudgy little guy with the high-school-dance haircut and squeeze-toy voice."

"He wants only adoring blondes half his age around him."

"As dramatically opposed to your boss," said Maurizio. I smiled but couldn't quite manage a laugh.

We stepped over to where the bar was set up, and Maurizio asked, "Now, are you going to tell us who that was around your neck when you walked in the door?"

"Her name is Devi. Well, one of her names is Devi. She has, I think, four first names. I met her in line for an espresso at Café Venus. Another of her names is actually Venus."

"She should use that name," Eric said with a light shove to my chest. "It describes her. Or is she somehow charmingly unaware of that?"

"I did bring it up. She told me that over time there have been different representations—the word she used was 'embodiments'—of Venus and said she didn't identify with them all."

"Are you together?" asked Maurizio, obviously trying to reconcile what was taking place across the room.

"Does it look like it?" I said, then quickly followed with a remark to the effect of "I like the new apartment," not at all wanting to concern him with the grade-school drama playing out at his party. In truth, I was barely conscious of the surroundings and had to have a look around to make sure the observation wouldn't be taken as a slap.

"Thanks," he said. "It's a straight shot down Sutter, ten minutes to the office. I rollerblade it, which is helpful, because it's 4:00 a.m. and half the trip is through the Tenderloin … or, as the advertisement for the vacancy described it, 'Lower Nob Hill.'"

"How we all think of it," I said, acknowledging the reference. In San Francisco, in the nomenclature of the day, if "lower" or "outer" were attached to the name of your neighborhood, you didn't always live where you wished other people believed you lived.

Eric poured something from a shaker and handed it to me. We clanked and drank and talked awhile longer, the music drowning us out at times. Every so often I glanced toward Devi. The back of her left hand had come to rest lightly upon her new friend's forearm. She seemed catastrophically absorbed. It took more of an effort than it should have, but after several attempts I reassembled the words, *You are motion without form, life without color, safely apart the stormy isle.* I knew where I had heard them: in Cognitive Theory, only days before, the summer class I had enrolled in to sew up my missing science credit at State. Our cloyingly literary-minded professor recited them from a poem during a lecture on the biomechanics of the eye. He was advancing the argument that we dwell, for the greater part, in the amber of others' peripheral vision, and how only in this respect are we ever perceived objectively. I wondered what he might say about this moment: perhaps that I had rotated for now out of Devi's paracentral world. But also that something redeeming ought to come of it.

Eventually a pair of hands swept from behind my head and covered my eyes. "Guess who?" came a voice I was familiar with but couldn't immediately place. "You creep! You didn't recognize me because I'm not supposed to be here."

"You're right about that," I admitted, scanning the room.

"Don't worry, she's not here," Jen said. "But if she were, she would tell you not to neglect Princess Sita over there."

"So that's what I'm doing," I said, crestfallen Gail hadn't come and at the same time conscious of the absurdity of feeling that way. It would have only intensified my disgrace.

"Are you and Maurizio—?" I half asked. He and Eric had stepped away.

"Yesnomaybe. Next subject."

"I don't have another subject right now."

It took all of that brief exchange for Devi to appear next to me and run her hand up my rib cage. Her attentiveness, I knew, was only indirectly related to me, so I introduced her to Jen. That lasted a few minutes and then Devi and I were alone.

"She seems nice."

"She's great," I said and left it there, aware she wanted to know more.

"That guy I was talking to, Archer?"

"Archer?" I couldn't remember the guy's name and was surprised when I heard it. Then again, it would have been unreasonable to expect him to actually go by Prick.

"Yes. He's so funny!"

"Yeah, he's hysterical. I'm cracking up right now."

"What?" she said, letting her arm fall.

"Nothing. Hey, what can I get you?" I asked, pulling her toward the bar. "Or are you still interested in skipping out of here?"

"Let's stay awhile," she said with an air of utter non-commitment toward anything. Devi, I was learning, while apparently habitual in the need to keep her options open, had no talent for the nuance of it. Typical for a guy, strange for a girl.

"So, how do you know Jennifer?" she asked.

I thought about it—rather, I assumed an attitude of having thought about it, for the words had lined up right away—and said, "Well, she and Archie—Archer, I mean. They've been together." And even as I spoke, the question unfurled itself in the air, *Is this why you haven't sustained a relationship since Gail or because of it?* It seemed important to decide, yet was too fraught an issue to immediately work through. The prospect that Gail, or having been with Gail, or having lost Gail, had marked me in some way, caused me to self-destruct with all women who had come after: it would mean a connection between us remained, one through which only grief could travel.

"You don't mean that," she said, unable to suppress a faint look of panic, already colocating the two of them in the room, arcing them together. Again, it was almost laughably lacking in subtlety.

"Well, who knows what's going on now, right?"

She stepped back. She took in the sum of me, then focused directly in on my eyes: hovering near but not quite inside comprehension of the lie. In that instant, perhaps more so than any other, I appeared front and center, awash in subjectivity.

Quietly she asked for directions I didn't have, then veered off in search of a bathroom. I hesitated a moment, then headed for the door. We had been there less than an hour. On the way out, I shouldered roughly past trader dude and at the last instant caught Jen's eye. I walked over to her.

"What?" she said.

"I don't suppose you'd consider not saying anything to Gail."

She didn't respond right away. When she did, she said, "There, I've considered it. No."

"Nice."

"I'm just being honest. You want me to be honest, don't you?"

"Is she seeing anyone?"

She drew a finger across her lips.

"It's not that I don't care for you," she said. "It's just that I am clear where my allegiances lie. Aren't you?"

"I'm not sure guys actually have allegiances. In the very end result, anyway. Women are mostly responsible for that, aren't they?"

She answered by not answering, then said, "So, what's about to happen here?"

"I'm a little spent."

"From what I have been told, this is all too familiar. Are you sure you want to do this? She's exquisite."

"What have you been told? That might help me resolve a few things. I'm feeling a bit unlucky."

"That you're … unfair, basically. That you expect others to be definitive when you are not. That you half commit to everything. That you'll walk away at the moment which can be least justified. Do you want me to go on?"

"So, then. I shouldn't hold out for another chance."

Over a faded "Day on the Green" tee shirt, chosen at the last second for its evocation of a shared memory—an expression of sentimentality that would forever go unappreciated—I wore an open, flagrantly unironed button-down Oxford. She gathered both sides of the shirttail in her hands and said gently, plaintively, "Nothing … nothing could ever make that happen."

"Yeah, I know," I said and accepted her no-hard-feelings kiss on the lips.

Devi caught up with me in the stairwell. I had hung back too long with Jennifer.

"You were just going to leave me here? How would I have made it home?"

"I wasn't really thinking about it."

"Jeff, what's wrong," she said, soft and cajoling, not really a question, and there she was, sliding up my chest again. It seemed impossible and inevitable at the same time. As she tipped up to kiss me, I shucked out of her grasp and said, "Come on, Devi. I'll take you home."

We drove off in silence. It was dark but not late, the city was lit up, sidewalks were streaming. Crowds loitered in front of clubs, restaurants, and Muni stops, and traffic stopped and stuttered as drivers sought to visualize parking into existence. Devi sat snailed-up on the far edge of the passenger seat, her gaze set out the window.

I felt aggrieved by the conversation with Jen. *Not definitive*—Gail had said that and never explained it, and I wouldn't have bothered to ask her to. Such was our relationship in its final days: dispassion, or the habits that describe it, elevated to the highest, most connotative art. Who between us could affect the purest absence of remorse over what had, at times, been a relationship with a certain desperate necessity to it.

Ah, you need to let it go, I nearly said out loud, then devoted myself for the remainder of the drive to getting back to where I started out that evening, the original state of mind. It was crude, I was aware of it then, and the six-year age difference seemed significant in context. But I didn't want to pass up the chance to reach the natural state with Devi if the chance were truly there. I felt so whipsawed from the back-and-forth with her, on the first date and now the second: it calmed me to focus on that one thing.

I jumped a low curb across from her place. We sat there awhile, still not talking—each, I imagine, bearing down on our own fatally-at-odds determination about what had to happen next. Eventually I stepped out, circled the car, reached her just as she closed the door behind her. As she turned to leave, I extended an arm toward the window glass, then bracketed her with my free arm as she spun the other way. She would fall into me now, I was sure of it, each of us forgiven, the stops and starts behind us linking to an unbroken chain carefully laid through to that moment. I waited, the night eddied, and slowly, slowly, yet still not slow enough for me to fully comprehend, she bowed her head and caped her arms inward, a seabird folding into sleep. I pressed against her, tried to find her mouth, but she wrenched, twisted, tried to pull away. The more she struggled the faster I held on, the more insistent I became. It's difficult to describe where I was at this point: not, as is evident, on the continuum toward accepting that Devi no longer wanted this to happen, but also not in denial; not lodged in disbelief. I was trying to catch the glass before it shattered; roll beneath the descending steel door.

After almost certainly less time than I had a sense of, she broke free, or I let her go, or her fury found the tension point at which I cracked into an awareness, finally, of what I was doing, of what she must have believed I meant to do next. And then off she ran, ran for her life, her hair pennanting behind her, heels typewriting across the asphalt. She flashed past the baffled light escaping from the first-floor window of her building, then swept like an unfinished brushstroke through its front door, the hydraulic hinge taking long enough to clamp shut so that a pursuer, any pursuer so inclined, could have crossed the street and slipped in after her. But I had done enough, hadn't I? *Haven't I, Gail? Definitive at last. Standing firm while another ran.*

The air had turned cool, a single sodium globe burned at the corner, and not very far away a Muni rail car scored through a curve of track. "If ever there was a time," I spoke to the lamppost and the letter box, "If ever there was a time," aware even then it was a strange thing to summon, never mind the circumstances. But it was a vacant thought. I never had learned to stand on my head.

We were parked alongside a highway access road a few miles south of Chula Vista. George held up the vial with the illicit contents he had brought along on the trip. It was out of the question we approach the border with that still in the car.

"I can't throw this away," he said.

"All right," I said. "Then have what you want now, and dump out the rest."

"That would be—how can I put it—impossible."

For a quiet half minute, he twirled the vial at his finger-tips. There was a slender, daisy-stem structure to George's wrists and hands, an image likely imprinted upon me just at that instant.

"'Impossible' may imply a corporeality which isn't there," he said by way of reconsideration. "A barrier of physics. How about this: in the realm of ideas, it cannot be accommodated."

No, of course it couldn't. I understood as much, despite my unhelpful suggestion to the contrary. If the powder inside the tube was not an attraction for me—it wasn't—then there were varied enough obsessions in my life to recognize the value assessment. This brought me, after a moment of deliberation, to a practical decision: I would share the cocaine with George because what remained might be enough to kill one person, though probably not two if it were split.

We took care of the matter in a single fifteen-minute gorge, then sat back to let the weather system pass through us. Getting any effect from it took a while and never really found a crescendo, at least for me. An attack of nose needles and a refrigeration of the circuitry in the upper half of the brain. I noticed a little chest pressure and had the sensation of a dry chemical mist suffusing the confined air, which almost certainly was real. I had one prior experience to compare it to, and this felt about the same.

Eventually I stepped out of the car, in need of open space. George emerged a moment later. It was a grim, featureless stretch of straight, bleached road. Gravel from the shoulder lay scattered about the landscape from a thousand instantly forgotten tire swipes. A moil of yellow dust eddied at our ankles, like a fog too lazy to float. Dense, clotted daylight lay spread across the sky, so that to pinpoint the sun required focus and patience enough to adjust—attributes difficult to come by at that precise moment.

George caught me looking up and said, "They sent an astronaut from Mexico along on the last shuttle mission, I'm pretty sure."

"That's not what I was trying to validate."

"It's strange, isn't it? Over time we've sent up one of every subtype, and if we haven't we will—by nationality, race, gender, religion, sexual preference. And then that individual, among his or her collective, is intended to embody a certain hegemonic pride. But there will always be the essential humiliation of having sent up a monkey first."

"I thought a dog went first," I said, evidently too mumbly to interrupt his flow.

"It's a metaphor for evolution."

"That's a bit of a stretch."

Just then, a beaten-up stake-bed coasted by with a cluster of engines and transmissions strapped to pallets in the back, no doubt headed for a junk rebuilder operation across the border. Fifty yards or so beyond us it stopped in the middle of the road. A barrel-shaped guy jumped out of the passenger side and short-legged it back our way. Reaching us, he circled the car, slowly, regardfully, crouching at each corner to train his eyes down the length of the body, let them dwell there. In one hand he held what appeared to be a substantial wad of U.S. currency in a tarnished silver clasp.

George's car on any day was an unusual sight: an unrestored, two-door relic from the sixties, something called a Plymouth VIP. I had never noticed another, anywhere. For that matter, I had never seen anything on the road with such vast expanses of unseamed sheet metal. The doors were massive and swung like the gates to a livestock pen. The hood and deck lid were studies in pure prairie flatness.

At last the guy approached us. We had drifted off the paved surface by then, though no other traffic had come.

He extended the hand with the money in it and gestured toward the car. A stuttering, three-way conversation ensued, predominantly in Spanish, during which there flared up a kind of contagious toeing of the earth. We understood it had ended when the guy jammed in a final, exclamatory divot and chugged off toward the truck.

"I think he offered fifteen hundred," I said.

"He did."

"He didn't appear to take it too well. That you wouldn't sell."

"I don't know if you caught that part at the end."

"Not entirely."

"Something along the lines of, if we take this particular vehicle much farther south, we'll be selling it for free."

"No, I didn't get that," I said, then made an effort to work back through the jumbled last seconds of the exchange before deciding to let it go. It felt like it was time to get back in the car. Neither of us made the move, though, and after a lull George said, "I'm thinking of staying awhile this time."

I didn't answer or bother to look his way, having nothing helpful to say on the matter. George needed to alter his circumstances, that was clear, and the entire trip and the period leading up to it was shaded by a sense of him shoving off from what was known and fixed in his life. He hadn't worked in weeks, drawing down his huge bank of stored-up vacation with the city; had stopped writing long before and, as far as I could tell, disengaged from the theatre, his friends there, the projects he was involved in. For the most part, he remained shut away in his flat, drinking, toking on his shell pipe, and, I now had the picture, dosing himself by other means as potent or more so, though not even I—really, probably only Regina—had any true idea about the extent of it.

Standing there, in that sad, scrubland emptiness, no breeze, nothing moving around us, I became conscious in a way I never had before of the ten years or so separating George and me, seeing it as a measure of time I had to work with until my own life reached some similar point. It didn't make sense, the two of us were so unlike each other. Yet, he was for me in that moment quite literally a wreck on the side of a road. I couldn't help but project myself into it.

He went on to say, "I don't know for how long, maybe a few months. I think that's all I'm allowed without a visa," and it registered for me that he had given consideration to his return, that he wasn't headed down there with the idea of living out some tragic, literary end to things. *Too derivative for his artistic sensibilities*, I thought a little ruefully.

"Welp, I should probably head back anyway," I said and launched into a gigantic, ripping body-stretch, a joint-cracking, endorphin-releasing stretch of the kind I have caught myself uncorking over the years when a complete change in direction is about to take place.

"You can still come. I didn't mean to say you couldn't. I just thought I should tell you."

"I understand. But I'm going back. Work and other things, you know?" I said, though given how I felt at that moment, work was the least legitimate excuse I could have offered. I knew where I had to go and who I needed to see and, transgressor that I had become, was turning myself around at the border. George and I had completed for each other the favors our friendship at the time required, even if unintentionally: I had accompanied him near to his destination, in one piece and contraband-free; he had reminded me that however brightly the sun shined along the Baja coast and however warm the water, I would find no refuge there from the condition that had led me to take off with him in the first place. Three weeks had passed since the second-date disaster with Devi, and I had dreamwalked through nearly every day since.

Two hours later, I sat in the back of an air-conditioned Scenicruiser headed toward L.A. and north from there, tallying up all the cowboy hats lying on the overhead racks, thinking, *There must be a vastly higher percentage of them here than you'll find in the general population.* George would have passed through the border by then, finishing alone this time the spur-of-the-moment trip we had taken together on a couple of other occasions over the years. I had advised him as a sendoff not to get busted for drugs in Mexico, trying to gauge for a final time the depth of his self-destructiveness. He just laughed.

Later, rolling up I-5, in a glimmer of consciousness in the midst of a long, drooling nap, I communed, if didn't exactly say, *George, this machine rides just like your car. You should've taken the fifteen hundred.*

A wooden chock held open the front door to the four-story stucco, a slathered, not-altogether-upright structure, the stand-up drunk propped between two slightly less besotted companions. An unmarked van stood at the curb, and some type of pump or generator thrummed inside of it. A long, flexible tube snaked out the back and up the stairs, and it twitched and torqued alongside me as I followed it up to Devi's apartment. Inside, I found a slender guy with a ponytail, very young, leaning on the rigid stem of a vacuum hose, smoking. He straightened up when he noticed me, and, as he did, a petal-burst of ash fluttered from his stub to the damp carpet. He let his eyes wander, as if to disown it, then slid out the hose and sucked it in.

"Are you the landlord?" he asked.

I hesitated, wondering how anyone could project onto me the authority necessary to appear to be the owner of an eight-unit rental property in San Francisco. "I'm not the landlord," I told him.

"Good, good," and then, a few seconds later: "Wiffler. Bizarre name, huh?"

"Sorry?"

"The landlord. That's his name. Sounds like a Batman nemesis, doesn't it? '*The Wiffler*,'" and at that he slashed a W-figure into the air, first with one arm, then the other, letting his equipment drop to the floor.

"I'll have a look if it's okay," I said and skirted around him, not waiting for an answer. I walked into Devi's room, empty; glanced behind her roommate's door, a girl with cropped, chestnut hair who I'd seen only from the back as she swished around a corner the one time I was invited up. Everything was gone.

I retreated downstairs and rang the bell to the unit below. It opened after nearly a minute of complete yet somehow not abandoned silence. A guy about George's age, also of mixed origin, though perhaps more of an Atlantic versus Pacific strain, waited for me to speak. He emanated a kind of slack, ballasted neutrality. I felt my presence there wasn't a surprise to him, without being able to say exactly how or why.

"Mind telling me where Devi is?" I asked.

He looked to the side, grazed his knuckles along the doorjamb. Biding his time, he said, "A couple of weeks ago some guys took away her things. Four or five Indian guys. She left sometime before that. So, no. I really couldn't tell you."

The information circled my consciousness for a moment before it bored in, connected with what she had confided to me months earlier … *they'll kidnap me if they ever find me.* I stepped across from him into the open foyer—not because I believed she was there, I didn't, but out of some need to acquire a better view of the context; of the three-sixty around her.

Along the length of one wall stood columns of unpainted plywood cubes filled with books and recorded music. There was a rack of audio equipment I recognized as very high-end. I panned around to a series of mounted charcoal drawings, hung level at the bottom and at fixed intervals in the style of a gallery display. Three were of Devi, and I found it difficult to look away. The shape lines were dense and heavily shadowed, yet lay unconsolidated upon the paper as if they could lift off in fragments at the slightest disturbance. The images were heartbreaking in the way art often strives to be.

I hadn't resolved what to say to Devi had I found her there. Certainly nothing with the intent of reclaiming her or appealing to her sense of forgiveness. You have to believe, first, that that's being a reasonable thing to ask, and I didn't. If a certain ambition had brought me there, and even at the time the notion seemed an imprecise one, it was to try to overwhelm what had happened, see it drowned under some other redeeming truth she might take in. I had come with nothing, nothing at all to offer, no poetic or graphic appreciation of her, no material relief for her predicament, no obvious recommitment to simple decency, not that any of those would have helped. When I arrived and discovered her gone, the answer was given to me, even if deep in my veins the first apperceptions of irrationality and hopelessness immediately pushed off and began to circulate: I would rescue her. I would find her and bring her back and set her free. And that, finally, was what she would have in her mind about me.

On the front landing, I found Sig smoking, Carpet Kid talking. I heard him say, "You should check out the pile on this thing, it's kelp." And then, acknowledging my presence, "He's seen it. It gets so you can't even boil it clean." He filleted out another less-elaborate jujitsu move then, strictly for my benefit.

I said to Sig, "What about the roommate?"

He shrugged, barely, and in that faint gesture I could see he was beyond all this; had reached a point of completion with Devi, an attainment for my own account that now lay thousands of miles and half an ocean away.

I knew none of her friends, so there was no one to call. I returned to her apartment hoping to find her roommate's name still on the intercom, discovered it blank. I attempted to track down Wiffler, but he hardly seemed to exist, and I had to resist any attribution to him of villainous intent or comic surreality. He was a landlord, that's all, and endured in the faraway sense of any big city landlord.

There were other bases I thought to cover. I phoned the office where she worked and learned that she no longer held employment there but nothing more. Resorting to a stakeout, I cornered a co-worker of Devi's who I knew to be in her circle, having met up with them once at a lunch spot on Kearny Street—this, in the aspirational days before our first date. She relayed the slightly less official line that Devi had quit, moved away, though she was at a loss to confirm if the information was delivered to the company by Devi or a surrogate. She appeared anguished and kind, and I had the feeling, in this instance only, that Devi listened as we spoke, as if she remained close to this girl in a metaphysical sense—the kind of blacklight-and-beads garbage I almost never tolerated at the time, especially because of the city in which I lived.

As a final measure, I stopped by Café Venus and inquired with the owner, who also worked the espresso bar, and who had comped her an *americano* and spoken to her in a paternal way on the day I met her there—"only because of my dumb name," she laughed, but I took from this that it happened as a matter of course. This guy, always more soapboxer than barista, he recited the canonical line, "I know one thing, that I know nothing," and commenced wondering aloud what my angle was.

To be clear, throughout it all, I had it fully within me that Devi was in Fiji. The few words Sig had let drop had settled safe and well-ordered in my mind. I had only to follow where they led. But a certain due diligence needed to take place—deliberate, thoroughgoing steps I saw as part of, or inseparable from, the hygiene I practiced every day, the commitment that in my years in San Francisco it had become essential for me to make: to not do the desperate thing; to know where the float-level lay in the city and stay above it. The bridge jumpers, the trolls in the park, the lost, barefoot kids on Haight Street; the wild-eyed Jesus claimants at Powell and Market and the solemn, doomsday sign carriers in the Financial District; the ever present horde of the narcotized and the inebriated who made all of Civic Center a wasteland at the time, or, for that matter, the vultures who given the chance would prey on them; the flinching, muttering, overcoated grease pencils we'd get at the brokerage drumming out the same trading symbol a dozen times a minute; the profligates who showed up at every party and drank too much, puffed too much, blew too much; the sorry, ragged homeless everywhere—they had let themselves fall. They had been above the surface and had fallen, had forgotten or never learned or stopped believing that it took a conscious act not to succumb, not to lose yourself. The casualties were everywhere. It didn't matter if they were drawn to the city or created there. The virus had found its forgiving host. I couldn't live in their proximity, ride the Muni in the periphery of their stink, sift among them on the streets, share even a carpet and walls and water dispenser with them five days a week, take in the abject and outrageous one day only to take them in the next and the next in ever larger swigs, without willing myself apart, doing the necessary things at the necessary moments to remind myself I was not—would never be—one of them. Such as running down as determinedly as I could every slim chance Devi hadn't already left for Fiji. Somehow, as it must have gone for me then, the process alone was the qualifier; the act of discipline that salvaged the delusional intent. I would find her in Fiji? How? And return her to the U.S.? By what physical and legal means? Of course, the alternative was to do nothing. Do nothing and be glad the vector of my disgrace was stashed away on an island in the middle of the South Pacific. Perhaps forever. Perhaps in some sort of captive situation. But that was—would have had to seem to me then—the surer sign of my own descent.

I called Ezra. I didn't know how much money it would take but knew what I had wasn't enough. He said, "What's wrong with the car? You don't like the car? It's beautiful. You just bought it from me three months ago!"

"Six."

"Six, six. It's a beautiful car."

"It's a piece of shit. But that's beside the point. How much will you give me?"

"No, no, I couldn't. I can't take it. Impossible."

"It's beautiful, remember?"

"Beauty is one thing. Allocation of capital is another. Anyway, you still owe me a thousand."

"Seven-fifty. Which you can deduct."

"I'll take the car and forgive the thousand. Finished."

"Ezra," I said, accustomed by now to his side steps after years of causal interactions through a mutual friend. There was a price. There was always a price, as this is what he did, this is how he ate: bought and sold and pocketed the arbitrage, typically with cars picked up at auctions, as mine had been. He was divining as we spoke; weighing the *Ezra-as-a-lovable-guy* factor against whatever that had gained him or cost him in his recent deals and everyday shenanigans.

"Okay. Fifteen hundred. Fifteen hundred, my friend. That's my offer." *The same for George's yacht*. "But first we deduct the thousand."

And so it went until we settled on twelve-fifty, net. I'd have taken less.

The next day, cash in hand, and at Ezra's direction, I met up with a fare consolidator—one in his vast network in the funny-business game. After ticking off a handful of options, she presented me with the only affordable one: flying as a courier rat.

"What's that?"

"You're allowed a seat on the plane and the space underneath. That's all. They use your weight allotment for small freight." She was a florid, near perfectly oblate woman with arrowpoint eyes who cast a glowing, adamantine presence behind her computer screens.

"I can do that."

"And you won't have a set day. You have to be ready to leave on twelve hours' notice."

I paid her in full before leaving her office, which Ezra had told me to expect, and went about taking care of a few last things.

I got in touch with Regina, even though I doubted she'd be much interested in what I had to tell her. "You just left him there?" she said after a measured pause and with a flourish of deft, experimental accusation. I felt the graze of the insult and then an immediate cauterization around the wound. If George needed me to save him, he would, at that juncture, have had to visit me in my dreams and retrain my compass. Which assuredly he would try before appealing to Regina for help.

"I'm just letting you know, Reg. Not to expect him back, like, tomorrow." Her little kid sang and chattered in the background, an off-key accompaniment to an immediately strained conversation.

"You know, Jeff," she started in, then waited for me to prompt her further, which my learned mistrust of her would not let me do. She finally continued, "George really cares for you. Really, really cares for you. You have no idea."

I tried to go blank, said something like, "Yeah, whatever," before hanging up on her. Regina's inference was clear and goading, and I had long had a sense of George's conflicted sexuality. Yet it never had and never would become an issue for us, I was certain. I should have called her back that day and blasted her but made the terrible mistake of phoning Rhys instead.

"So, you were going to be out for five days and it's been ten. You didn't call. You didn't return my calls—until now. We're here without any idea as to whether or not you've quit, you're in a hospital, you're dead, you ran off with a hotel maid in Mexico—"

"I never got to Mexico."

"I'm delighted to hear it. Who knows how much longer we would have had to hover by the phone, waiting for you to grace us with a speck of common decency. Is this your way of bucking for a promotion, Jeffrey?"

There were times—brief, clear remissions in the progression that extended from the moment of having decided to go to Fiji to the act of boarding the plane—when I saw it all. The preposterousness of the task. The repudiation of my own commitment to propriety set against the methodical planning I meant to pass for it. The forsaking of whatever stability I had managed to fashion in my life. The self-serving intent of all that I was doing. This would become the most starkly set-off of such times.

"I have to leave," I told him. "For a couple of weeks," I added, because I knew from the ticket lady that my first chance to depart was several days out, and to catch a return, a week beyond that.

"Leave? How mysterious. How importunate. Jeffrey, allow me to try again. It appears—I would go so far as to describe it as an ineluctable fact—that you already have been gone for a couple of weeks. That is: You. Already. Did. Leave."

"I apologize, Rhys. There is something I have to take care of, though."

Silence. The silence of static, contemplative breathing; over a gingerly held phone; through febrile, gull-wing nostrils. A soft half-smile, one he could never quite tighten, lingering even at a moment like this. His backwards-tapering figure held primped and toplofty behind his desk. "Okay, Jeffrey. Fine," he said. "Best wishes on your quest for the light. But please, do this. You might want to consider the possibility—just take it into consideration—that you won't have a job waiting for you when you return. From wherever."

"I'm not too worried," I both said and affected. "I could always suck your cock and get it back," an at-least conceptual truth made untrue by the speaking of it, a consequence neither taxing to accept nor perhaps even unintended. I needed to make it final. To deliberately miss the apple with the thrown knife and impale the thing beneath it. Have it so that the last of what there was to let go of, the job, the benevolent boss, would be gone. Ezra had the car. Booze, drugs, and now Mexico, my closest friend. Someone else almost certainly had my one significant love, for whom, in the two years since we had broken up, I harbored the most repressed, long-shot desire, and now not even that … *Nothing* … *nothing could ever make that happen.* And Devi, well, Devi had taken with her, whether having left voluntarily or not, the one possession for which I was willing to surrender all others: my stake in a basic sense of rectification I felt I couldn't move forward without;

which seemed indispensable to accomplishing certain rudimentary things. Such as having a relationship again. With anyone. Ever. Or having to explain to a plum-eyed boy of nine, emerging into an acute anthropological curiosity at the time I would write this story, about how, in all circumstances, he should behave with women, lines he should never cross, a conversation I might not have foreseen so much as registered as one among dozens of destinations on a deep-dream flicker board. At last, in a manner that would condemn it to the pile of irreducible regrets, and with a finality for which I may have had Regina to thank, I had left myself with zero reasons not to go. To retrieve what Devi alone could offer back to me.

As for the conditions under which Devi had left: couldn't she have refused, I wondered? Sought some kind of intervention? After all, she had to walk through an airport, board a flight, sit passively for hours, clear border entry on the other end. Possibly, it fell out for me in the drifting last days before my departure, her immigration status had come into play. Or an acculturated limit was reached in her capacity to refute parental authority, filial obligation. Or, it had to be considered, her resistance to such pressures was dismantled by her involvement over the years with any number of ill-intentioned jerks—me among them; Sig, I couldn't say. Ultimately such thoughts were overtaken by shame at how little I bothered to find out about her in the lead-up to our first date and on the two dates themselves.

On the day that notice of my flight came, I returned the lone message left unreturned since arriving back in town from the drive south with George. The conversation, I knew, would hew to a certain structure: she would ask the questions, I would answer, the exchange never venturing far from the reef-protected subject of my higher education, the central topic upon which, over the prior few years, an approximate familial and eventually even contributory connection had been reestablished. Yes, I had finished up with the summer class. No, there was nothing, as far I knew, that might imperil my graduation status—a lie, as my term paper was handed in late, and the deal the professor had offered, to dock me a full grade, I hadn't yet accepted (convinced, as I was, that I couldn't afford the penalty). On this call, as it happened, she informed me that my father had sold his decades-old, surnamed electrical contracting business, and I did, in fact, experience a reflex of—not lament, not relief, not—well, there is no word for it. For a moment, I wound it back, way, way back to the early consciousness days, when the family narrative involved my working for him, then with him, then continuing on with it myself, and it had all been magical to think of. This, before the years of rage and resentment intervened. His, the first; mine, the second. "Good for you both," I said, or something not too different, and assured her I would call again soon with news about school. A day and a half later, I landed in Nadi, at which point a coup led by a high-ranking Fijian colonel, those of his superiors unsympathetic to the cause impaneled through no accident off the main island, was already set in motion.

The bus came to a stop in a scattershot town an hour or so drive past the capital city. Within minutes, most of the islanders aboard had dispersed, including the driver. "There is a fresh disturbance in the government," the woman seated next to me had replied when I inquired some fifty kilometers back if that wasn't Suva we were leaving in our wake, putting into context, as much as she could or felt obliged to, the several chaotic military roadblocks we had passed, the intermittent bursts of sirens, the smoke floating up from what must have been part of the city center.

Where we finally pulled over wasn't a terminus so much as a place where buses idled, the telltale assortment of seedy commissaries arrayed nearby. The clearing in front was bare and tire-sluiced, and dunes of trash rippled out toward the perimeter. An abandoned ticketing kiosk stood off to one side, and against it leaned the Australian couple I had chatted with on the flight from L.A. and again before setting out from the airport in Nadi. They were, I had the impression, collecting information from anyone coming or going who might have it, so I walked over to listen in.

Our presence being a novelty there and evoking a kind of pity, we were guided after some minutes into an unmarked stall amid the jumble of tin roofed shops. Behind the counter, just above a shelf stocked with green, half-liter cartons of Milo, a television with a foil antenna faded in and out of signal. An officer in camos and a beret, of the sort all revolutionary leaders in the developing world see fit to drape themselves in, rambled on in an undulating tone and with grand, self-conscious gestures. He declared at one point, "God has expressed that Fiji must remain for the Fijians," to which Sam, the Aussie, barracked, "Well, that says it nicely, doesn't it? What other justification would you need?" I turned in time to see Beth, his partner, sink an elbow into his ribs that he appeared at least somewhat prepared for. It swept me back for a moment, even in that remote, bizarre context, toward some long-ago incident with Gail, though I couldn't quite bring it into focus.

I glanced around the small, crowded space we were in and scanned the other faces—all of them, I observed, of the native Fijian or non-Indo-Fijian type: the ones, I understood, with whom God had allegedly thrown in. There was no reading their reaction to what they were seeing and hearing, only that surprise was not a part of it. The air inside the shop was a fug of exhaled smoke and ripe, sweating fruit.

It became apparent after a while and a number of inquiries, for which I was only a bystander as my new and much more world-savvy companions patched together the situation, that passage into Suva would be inadvisable if not altogether unmanageable for the next several days—a realization I gave into reluctantly and nearly too late before agreeing to split a ride with them back to Nadi. Devi's family, I was sure, lived in Suva, and I was desperate not to backtrack. A good chunk of my determination had dropped away somewhere over the Pacific, and I had become uncomplicatedly aware of the futility of nearly all I meant to accomplish by making the trip. Giving up ground in any amount could be fatal.

The return trip across the island was hellish. The driver we hired insisted on a northern route to steer clear of the trouble in Suva, and it devolved into hours of body-slamming travel over cratered roads through a deeply blackening night. At times I doubted we were even on a road, and it seemed miraculous that the wreck we were in, a blanched, two-tone Land Rover, didn't flip or crack open as we bottomed out time and again. Halfway into the journey, we stopped so the Aussies could roll fresh cigarettes. I was beyond exhaustion from the sleepless, nonstop travel over the prior two days and literally dropped to my knees outside the truck while waiting for them to finish. Over the tobacco floated a floral scent, a little more pleasant, breaking in waves from somewhere near or far. I couldn't identify it then but would a couple of months later, offered on a cool, rainy afternoon and with blithe sincerity a cup of hibiscus tea, and experience the same momentary tinge of alleviation.

Sam and Beth, they seemed indefatigable to me: not untired but conditioned to weather all blows, as if travel were all they knew—an assumption I would learn was true, in a figurative sense, Fiji being their twentieth or thirtieth stop on an open-ended circumnavigation of the globe. By the time we rolled into Nadi, they had settled on an island-hop to Rarotonga where they would wait until things cleared up in Fiji, or didn't. They asked me to go with them—to "come with," Beth said, absent the pronoun and any hint my tagging along would at all be an exceptional development. That night, or for what was left of it, and a good part of the next day, I crashed on the floor of the cheap hostel-like room they had quickly found with the help of the driver. Despite my angst over just about everything, and with only a jute mat as separation from the clay tiles, I slept the oceanic sleep of the lower latitudes, waking at last when a worker entered the room to clean it.

Once my head cleared, I made my way to a travel bureau through which the courier tracked all its ticket holders. I was to update my contact information, in-person or by phone, whenever my coordinates changed. But there was a notice for me stating, in effect, that due to security concerns and their bearing on corporate liability, the company was moving out at once all its "casual agents"—their proper term for us, I learned just then. It seemed crazy; wildly overcautious. Other than small groups of armed soldiers here and there, there were hardly any signs in Nadi, the country's second largest city and only international embarkation point, that anything at all was going on. My first thought was to ignore the notice—despite Sam and Beth's offer, I intended to stay and try again for Suva in few days. But the message went on to explain that my visa was specific to my travel status and would be revoked should I not comply with the courier's directives, which would be forthcoming.

"That's a load of crap," Sam said when we met up again that evening, to which Beth replied, "Perhaps, but look, his document is a bit different," comparing the slip affixed to my passport to the one in hers. They were camped out at an open-air café next to the hotel, enjoying a meal and drinking the local bitter, both of which they immediately offered to share. Over the course of that round and several others, Sam settled on the view that with a girl involved he'd press on and do whatever he wanted, upheavals in government notwithstanding. "It'll all mix up to something, Jeff," he said at one point, "Jeff" sounding more like "Jiff" and the perspective reminding me an awful lot of George's, though perhaps less in the vein of offering counsel than egging me on. I hadn't fully explained to them why I had come to Fiji, only that I meant to catch up with a friend, but Sam had it in sight that there was more to the situation.

"Not having proper documents in a country in the midst of a military takeover," Beth said with an oblique, over-and-back neck-turn I had already identified as a signature of hers. "That wouldn't be the best thing, Sam, would it?" Her hair lay intricately knotted atop her head, and a kind of fantail sprouted from it that quivered when she spoke and gestured.

Sam shrugged and said, "Yes, but what would be the price? A little trouble with Passport Control on the way out, that's the very worst. As I see it, he should find the girl and have a go with her." And then, slinging a wide smile my way through his ragged, auburn beard and the smoke from his rollie—"Live it out to the end, Jiff. You can meet up with us in the Cooks in a week's time and cheer us with how you fared."

Later, back at the hotel, a fax awaited with my return itinerary to the U.S. By this time in the evening, my head was circulating a swill of weakly hopped ale and all manner of extreme travel stories, the disastrous or near-disastrous vivid among them: shitting out worms in Nepal; sleeping with rats in Goa and snakes in Chiang Rai; nearly capsizing while on a pontoon boat a mile from shore in the South China Sea; Beth being locked up with hookers just inside the southern Thai border and having to bribe her way out; Sam stumbling into a sewage culvert in Tunis, then being laid up for weeks with a raging infection in his leg. "And then there arrived the day," Sam had said after we drained our bottles for a final time, reflecting in such a way that it may as well have happened a lifetime ago, "that we chanced upon, on Christmas Day, in a park in Madrid, two boys, one with a cape and the other with horns," Beth producing from her small, colorfully-stitched string purse, no doubt acquired at some far-flung village market, the photo she had captured of the young toreadors at play. It was then or in the moments after or at the very instant I stood in the hotel lobby trying to assimilate my departure date as the day after next, yet unable to get free of the image in the photo as a clarified last drop of all I had taken in that evening, that a wedge began to open into what I considered possible: possible in the context of a lived life; of the world as it was credible to me. An almost surreal dimensionality seemed to refract from decisions laid out in front of me, beginning at that moment and extending into the far future, which left selecting among them appear both fate-determinant and pointless.

I stayed. I returned to Suva. I never came close, to my knowledge, to connecting with Devi. In fact, over the course of several days in the city, I managed hardly any unencumbered interaction at all with Indo-Fijians, what with the ongoing tensions, the curfew, the vandalized or burned out or otherwise shuttered shops from which they would ordinarily have been selling. And nothing so extraordinary happened by way of recompense, no near-death experiences, no snakes in my room, filthy as it was, only roaches too menacingly large to crush, an assortment of which I left trapped and idling beneath overturned pottery—in my most morose moments in the aftermath of the trip, a vibrating representation of yet one more situation left unresolved. On the flight back to U.S.—and yes, I was hassled extravagantly, not by Fijian immigration but by the courier's local agent who I had blown off the week before—I sat next to an Indian businessman, an older, genial man of the sort I had failed to make contact with in Suva, and in bits and pieces parceled out my story. In my memory of it, we were roughly equidistant from the shore we had left and the one we aimed for when he laughed, patted my wrist, and said, "By what you have told me, I would think she is as likely in India now as she is in Fiji."

Without a car, and in the absence of any direct Muni route, I often walked home from work. Even in the rain I would do this, as on the day I am now writing about, though it was a light, early November rain. Only two or so miles lay between the job site and the share rental I found in the Sunset after giving up the apartment in Hayes Valley—a place that was always a stretch to afford, Gail having arranged for it before dumping it on me in the breakup. The work was temporary and under-the-table: essentially a laborer's role with a small, non-union contractor renovating a bank out on Nineteenth Avenue. There was a lot of tear-out involved, as well as gathering and organizing materials, and pretty much constant cleanup: tasks, generally, dished off to the lowest guy. Here and there, though, I would help run conduit or rough-in wire, drop in fixtures, rig up switch boxes, and after a while it became known that I had considerably more facility with this work than did the hired apprentice on the job. As a result, the arrangement had upended somewhat, much to the resentment of the guy with whom I traded roles. That the skills came back so easily was a revelation to me. Apparently, years of enmity were no impediment to deep learning.

Not far from home, a car eased to the curb and waited for me to come even with it. There was Stephanie, peering out from that throttling, yellow Saab of hers, offering me a lift to "wherever you're going." One consequence of having lost control of things for a while was having become, in the aftermath, quite literal-minded, and all I could think of at first was how there were only a few blocks left to walk. Fortunately, I didn't respond right away, and, when I did, asked if she'd like to have a coffee somewhere. She thought it was a fine idea.

Because of the time of day, and perhaps for other reasons as well, the place we went to, Arturo's, was empty. The front door stood open, filling the room with fall bluster and making sure our coats stayed on. Instead of coffee, we decided to split a carafe of tea. I left it to Stephanie to sort through the options presented to us and choose which to order.

"Inviting in the weather must be part of the experience," I said.

"I love it here," she replied. "The baroque music, the brocade drapery, the swirling air. It seems haunted in broad daylight."

"You've just cleared away every image I've ever had of you, Stephanie."

"Really? How is that?"

I considered the improbability of this moment even happening and said, "Would it be okay if I don't explain?"

She smiled, pulled her hair back and let it go, then asked in a manner so lacking in guile as to make answering in good spirits obligatory, "So, what's with the workman's clothes and mini cooler?"

I laughed and said I'd left the brokerage and gone into construction for a while, then sketched in for her some of the more temporal aspects of finding myself back in the trades: the brute exertion, the break-time-governed days; the off-color humor and outrageous language.

"I'm not having the easiest time envisioning you in that setting," she said.

"You're not the first," I told her, offering a historical perspective, though she may not have picked up on that.

"How long is a while?" she asked, and I admitted I didn't know. Having worked with my hands every summer and every weekend throughout my adolescence had stayed with me, and falling back on that, upon true, hard work, felt right at the time. One less thing to regret, really. I always had carried a vague sense of shame to my jobs in an office. Still, I wasn't keen on a lifetime of physical labor and knew I would have to get serious again about a career. There was also the thought, which ebbed and flowed, of putting enough money together to travel. It hadn't occurred to me where or for how long, though catching up with George stood out as a first order of business. He had sent a single postcard—a picture of the Sierra Madre Occidental, blank on the back save for the cryptonym "Rodolfo Neri Vela." Soon after, I would again see that name, this time beneath an image in a blue NASA jumpsuit, the subject of a poster stapled to a wall in a Mission District taqueria.

The conversation floated along, never dove very deep but didn't falter or become strained. Stephanie said toward the end, "You haven't mentioned how the graft is holding," a reminder that she knew me foremost in a respect in which there lingered a certain pride of artisanship. It was a form of objectification to which I couldn't take offense, as it may have smoothed over our misfire of a year ago and allowed us to come together again. Considering my altered circumstances, and the timing, this being the beginning of the long, gray season of rain, well

… there was nothing expiatory in realizing this was luck I didn't deserve, but I did realize it. Later, going over the conversation, the first uplifting one I'd had in a while, and resorting perhaps too self-generously to half-acquired, still-ungraded knowledge for meaning, I also fell to this: that with Stephanie the theory didn't apply, and the center of her gaze was the safest island to attain. I certainly felt unjudged there, something I feared was lost to me in all future interactions with women. As it happened, we would get together on occasion in the coming months and years, and a reliable companionship evolved, even if we never explored its limits. This wasn't love, though it may have been belief, and wasn't that the higher standard?

Going back to that afternoon now. As the tea steeped between us, its decaying fragrance tapered upward, my consciousness met it halfway, and for a while I was far, far away, on my knees, in the pitch dark, searching for relief in any small quantity. "Jeffrey," Stephanie gently prodded, "you've flown off into space, haven't you," which did bring me around, though again only to the most prosaic of thoughts: that while the journey was there to be taken, it helped to belong somewhere first. That seemed a ways off.

SEEN AT ELEVATION

LOST HILLS ABBEY FOR SISTERS OF THE NAZARENE

As the suspension towers come into view, I glance back to take in Simon's reaction and can see that he's drifted off. Almost from the start he's loved riding up high, on bridges, elevated trains, even aerial trams as we discovered on a visit to Tahoe earlier this summer. He twirls his wrists and ankles in opposed shaft-and-gear fashion, and light collects in his already bright, outsized eyes. Missing the drive across will make him unhappy, and the nap won't be long, but I decide not to wake him. Brooke would be concerned with his schedule, I know, but the next few days will be a little off for him anyway.

A coil of morning fog remains caught below the ridgeline on the south face of the Headlands, though the sky above looks promising. There is a small, trapezist thrill to crossing this bridge on any day, but now it's mingling with the obligation to enjoy it in Simon's place and anticipation of the long weekend in front of us. With Brooke headed to L.A. to meet up with college friends, and her mother awaiting Simon's hand-off in Tiburon, we are all in for something of a break: from the city and from each other.

We flash past Vista Point and bank up the wide curves of 101 to the immediate north, then curl down the winding circuit toward the peninsula. The swept roadway, the cultivated slopes splashed with poppies, the blur of sleek cars along the same route, they waylay the town's pretension as a bohemia before delivering you there. Renata's cottage lingers in idle rebuke, salt-pitted and overgrown, a quaint ruin amid the double-lot rebuilds that rule her street. She has lived here since Brooke was a grade-schooler and would own it outright if not for entanglements with an assortment of characters who prevailed on her to collateralize their small-time business ventures. There are guys like that everywhere, I have come to realize, one ready to take the place of another as soon it is left vacant. And Renata has been an easy touch, from all I can gather, though Brooke can't talk about it without spitting fire. Still, here she sits on a dune of prize North Bay equity, as little as that might ever mean to her.

"Ready to go, Simi?" I ask, holding open the door for him. He yawns, blinks, worries his feathery brows, sensing he's missed something important, yet unable to immediately settle on what it is. There is a change that happens at this age, or even earlier: a lapse of faith in transmigration—faith that comes from so often falling asleep in one place and waking in another. One in a long line of grave injuries to the scope of imagination.

"Rena's house," he says.

"Yep," I reply.

"Rena here," he states more emphatically, and I get that I haven't shown the requisite appreciation of his discovery. Even so, I don't bite, taking the opportunity to administer the rare dose of undiluted male influence. He makes sure I register his frown, then pommels over the rail of his car seat and searches for the ground with one leg. A corroded, white El Camino sits in the driveway, and he drags his fingertips along its quarter-panel as we amble toward the front porch. I brush aside the creepers dangling from the eaves, and we knock and call out, but no answer comes, so after a minute we let ourselves in. And there, it is immediately apparent, stands the owner of the ancient automotive centaur Simon has just measured off.

Tall, lashed together, a living cut-out of faded denim; lank, gray hair past his shoulders; complexion strafed by years in the elements. I have encountered this type over the years, possibly this very one. They tumble around San Francisco like the last leaves of fall, denizens of some obscure seam in the city or blown in from the hills, distinct for their faraway gaze, whippet appearance, and the lonely ambit around them, which we have just wandered into.

"Sorry, no one answered," I say, backing up a step, my hand on Simon's shoulder, Simon himself holding his ground.

"Why would I?"

"Pardon me?"

"It's not my house."

"Right … right. About that—"

"Renata?"

"Yes."

"She's gathering fruit."

"Pums," Simon murmurs.

"Pums?" the stranger says.

"Ah … plums, he's saying."

"Well then, plums it must be," he says and feints in Simon's direction. "And what is your name, helpful friend?

Mine is Lonny, which hasn't been a problem until now, but it does have an 'L' in it," and the introduction, while approximate to what anyone might direct toward a child, carries a note of deep unfamiliarity with the life-form. Simon weighs answering, weighs each element of what's going on, the presence of this individual in Renata's house, his aspect and tone, the stunted language between adults, the taut hand clamped over his collarbone. Evaluates it all in his steady, discerning way.

"I only know of one Lonny," I say, the words and realization arriving at the same instant.

"Yes, well, reputations," he sighs and allows his gaze to sweep the air above us. "Oft gained without merit, oft borne without gain."

Renata, in the wake of this exchange, drifts through the open French doors in back carrying a basket not of plums but Meyer lemons and says to Simon, "So, how does some fresh lemonade sound?" She hugs him with her free arm, rests her cheek against his, blows a kiss into the air … her chemo not so far behind her, still careful to avoid getting sick. Towing him along toward the kitchen, she lofts a welcoming glance over her shoulder, yet in a manner that almost dumbly ignores the grown man standing across from me.

"No, that's not right," he says with a flash of remonstration, and it takes me a second to realize he is contemplating the veracity of his own words, not the small transaction that took place in their aftermath.

"What is that from?" I ask, if only because his flight of thought seems to require it.

"Hmm, I'm not sure. I can't be sure it's from anything."

"Oh."

"Literature."

"Literature. That's a little broad."

"Probably shouldn't have said it," he mutters. "I never know what to say." And the remark, inescapably it seems, prefigures the moment that follows in which nothing is actually said. Renata and Simon's patter reaches us, interleaves with the breeze and birdsong floating in from the garden.

"Staying for lunch?" Renata inquires, leaning out from the kitchen, and again it hits me that she is not fully attendant to the current census in her own house. "Chemo brain," I can hear Brooke saying, lamenting, as she has so often lately, her mother's altered state, the blithe, disconnected air her treatment seems to have left her with—though I'm not sure that's the problem in this case.

"No, I have to get going," I say.

"Then I'll put a few things together and you can take them with you," she says and vanishes again.

"Where are you headed?" Lonny asks, and I am immediately relieved at the congruity of his question.

"Southern Oregon. Near Medford."

"Taking the coast?"

"Probably I-5. It's faster, isn't it?"

"That's your reason?"

"What?"

"Aw, hell. I don't know. I don't know if it's faster."

"I need to get up there," I say, trying not to sound dismissive, though it feels unnatural to grant him the courtesy. Any courtesy at all, really.

He turns and lopes away, passes through the double door and the arbor leading from the deck, then drops from view. Seeing him move, seeing his long, wicket frame and high strides, I recall one of the few things Brooke has let slip about him, from what little she knows, and this only from scrapbook clippings and stories relayed long ago by Renata: that he was a track star in high school, a state-level decathlete, and held a record for a period of time in the javelin throw. It is something, for now, that I can graft onto him, an attribute not entirely shaded by negativity. That and the essentiality of Brooke's existence. And of Simon's, by extension.

After a moment of indecision, I follow him outside. I find him kneeling next to a Buddha statuette, which lies partially submerged in the ground cover. Examining the engraving, he reads aloud in a low, charred voice:

The good renounce all,
pluck out desire,
abandon pride,
overcome all fetters.
Take the path of the sun, Wild Swan.
Life is a fine flower.

He falls into contemplation then, or some other exertion suggestive of contemplation. Half notes ping from a wood chime dangling inside the arbor. A beetle stumbles from the shadow of his gaucho-style hat, tries to keep purchase among the mint leaves. Finally, he says, "It veers off at the end there, doesn't it?"

"I never noticed. It sounds a little random."

"It wouldn't be like Renata to worry about such a thing."

"No."

"What about Brooke? She into spirituality and alternative lifestyles and all that?"

"Far from it," I manage to say, stung by the invocation of her name, aware that each word that travels between us separates me from Brooke and the sum total she has exchanged with him over the last twenty-plus years. It seems a terrible betrayal.

I head inside, ambush Simon from behind with a lift and a tousle. I tell him, "Don't make it hard for Rena," but it's unnecessary and earns a mute, restless shrug. He is an easy kid most of the time, except when Brooke and I argue, and then he has a way of amplifying the tension until we stop or one of us stalks off. As Renata hands me a paper sack weighted with provisions, it seems possible we'll have some sort of discussion about why exactly Lonny has shown up, how long he has been here, whether or not Brooke knows about it, what happens next. But it is utterly not my business. I should have nothing at all to do with it. When Brooke decides to tell me, that's when I'll get the story. And that's a pure preserve-the-peace decision, one I feel totally assured about the second it's made.

There is another awkward moment as Renata and I strategize our goodbye. I have found it harder to show affection to her since her diagnosis, which she can probably sense, though I never have been much of a hugger-kisser. Still, we get through it, and I can't help but notice how fragile she feels in my arms. Her hair is thin and tufted, her eyes glints of blue in a swirl of shadows, and there too I encounter difficulty, just trying to hold them steady. I wonder again if she is up to this—taking care of Simon for the weekend. But Brooke says it's time and is convinced it will be good for her.

As I head toward the car, Lonny emerges from the stone path leading from the back and yells, "Wait up!" Coming a step too close, he says, "My thinking is, why don't you swing by on the return trip? It's on your way. I live up north."

"I don't think so," I say after a moment of naked disbelief.

"I'm in Whitethorn, up in Humboldt. It's an easy detour. If you don't take I-5."

"I doubt I'll have time."

"Okay, okay. But look. I've got property up there. Someone should come and see it, just so they'll know. I tried to tell Brooke—or, no, I got word to Renata and Brooke a couple of years ago. Or maybe just Renata. But no one came. Someone should see it. I'm giving it to Brooke. Not right now, of course."

"I don't know what you're talking about."

"Brooke knows. Or Renata knows. It's a decent amount of land."

"Brooke thinks you're dead. Or she thought you were, when we first met. We haven't talked about it in a long time."

"Just thinks?"

"Pretty sure. But I can see how you'd wonder."

He draws back, adjusts his gaze, flicks off his hat so it loops down from his neck. He says, "Listen, take the Coast Highway. Before you hit Garberville, cut off toward Redway. Then head up the hill, twenty miles or so. When you get to town, ask for me. Ask how to get to Lon's place. It's a small town. It's not even a town. Ask the first person you see."

Sunlight filters through the maple near the curb, scatters at our feet. A squirrel barks at us from a rain gutter next door. We're impeding something, interrupting his rounds maybe. I distrust squirrels, and it makes me even more unbearably anxious to leave. I nod toward Lonny, or Lon, duck into the car, and peel off toward the interstate. It is my good fortune in this case that burning up the open road is a sport everyone here enjoys.

———

A call comes through as I exit a low-signal area south of Redding. Brooke enters mid-conversation, her voice mingling with others. It's a ghost-in-attendance moment, and I can tell by the laughter and high spirits she hasn't spoken with Renata. Eventually she says, "Jeff? Jeffrey?"

"Sounds like everyone is having a good time," I pipe up, taking aim for a gas station with an unmissable, double-pole sign tower. Mt. Shasta, fifty miles away, loses some of its stature as I pull closer, then vaults upward again as I slip beyond view of the sign.

"Oh, sorry. How long have you been there? I kept waiting for your voicemail."

"Not long," I assure her, and another several seconds of aural clamor go by during which I more or less construct the scene: oceanfront café, patchy mid-afternoon sunshine; cyclists, bladers, and skateboarders whizzing by; sand courts laid out in fencerows along the strand; everywhere the tawny plentitude of the L.A. beach set. This, plus a table of mothers in their thirties acting as though it all redounds to them, that they are youthful and carefree and inseparable from this vision. Then she says, "Can you please tell this guy you're my husband? That I actually am married?" A voice comes on with an extravagant and possibly not-even-authentic Latinate inflection and says, after identifying himself as Paolo, "Never, never my friend let such a woman out of your sight."

I wonder for a moment how Brooke, this far into our relationship, wouldn't know I'd be annoyed by this. And then I wonder, for the same reason, why I'm wondering. "Thanks for the advice," I tell him, and then add, without any real commitment to the idea, "but then how would I ever get out of hers?"

Much dimly heard perseveration ensues, and then it's Brooke again, "What did you say to him? He's just our waiter."

"Nothing that wouldn't eventually occur to you, I hope."

"Have you met up with your brother yet? Was Simi okay when you dropped him off?"

"He may not have noticed I left."

"I'm sure that's not true. Did you leave all his things with my mother?"

I hesitate a moment; attempt to visualize Simon's sleeping bag and duffel, carefully packed by Brooke, lying anywhere except in the trunk of the car …

"Uh, she may have to pick up a few items."

"Jeff …"

"Sorry. I was a little distracted while I was there. Do you want me to call her? Actually, she might want to hear from you. You should probably call."

"I was planning to. But I suppose that can't wait now."

"No, it definitely can. Just, at some point—"

"Ugh. I can't believe you forgot—wait, I can believe it. Of course I can." She leaves time for me to respond, but I have filled enough such openings over the years to realize I shouldn't. So she waits, waits a bit more, but perhaps a hard-won second less than the last time we had a standoff like this, and says, "Okay, so she's my mother. Mine to deal with, right?"

"That's the spirit," I say, trying to lighten things up a little.

She sighs, falls quiet, then picks up again with a slightly less afflicted tone, "Did you really forget everything?" But she knows there is only the single duffel, so we force a quick, determinedly-not-unpleasant goodbye. The odds are high I'll hear from her again soon. Minutes.

After gassing up, I open the sack from Renata. There is a jar filled with some sort of marinated grain with edamame and shredded carrots stirred in; a handful of raw almonds lying loose in the bottom; and two purple plums … plums, after all. These could be lean days for Simon unless she makes an exception to her current regime.

That much, to be sure, hasn't changed for Renata—the austere diets and the missionary zeal she brings to them. It is all of a piece for her and has been for even longer than Brooke can remember: rabbit foods and alt-medicines; eastern religions; spiritual tourism; the purifications of mind and body; the passion for whatever she is doing now and her unreflective dismissal of it when she moves on to the next thing. Cancer came into this as an affront, not only to her health but to her made image, her sense of equity and just rewards—so much so that she could only place it in the same construct, the same accommodating North Bay seeker aesthetic. Hence the purges, the aspirin baths, the mega-doses of custom vitamins, the radio-frequency treatments; the numerologist and the chant and meditation circles; the unilateral decision, just in the last week, to drop her post-chemo meds, which nearly sent Brooke over the edge.

I consider stopping for something less strictly inside the fodder-and-antioxidants realm but have reasons to keep moving—the most pressing so as to defensibly ignore Brooke's call. *Far better that my mind was on the road,* I can tell her later, and in the meantime she'll have had the space to cool down. Also, with hours of driving ahead of me, I need to make time. Daniel and I haven't planned out the weekend, but his girlfriend, Claire, is dancing tonight at some venue affiliated with the Britt, and we're expected to attend.

Slipping back onto the freeway, I experience the same twinge of unease as when I spoke to Daniel a few days ago. He has come out from Delaware to support Claire, whose troupe is on a shoestring tour of summer arts festivals. They have dated on and off for years, but she's based in New York now, in another world altogether, really. So there is an imbalance of a kind, or there is liable to be, and I don't have a great feeling about it.

Over the next several miles, I encounter every lowly variant of roadside fare, among them an In-N-Out Burger, the hardest to pass by. Perhaps as an escape from the cravings, or to relieve the monotony of I-5, I recall a long-ago road trip with a long-ago friend … in which the friend, a playwright of modest local lore, finding inspiration on a run south through the L.A. metroplex, conceptualized drive-throughs as linked along a continuum, which we traverse, Cheever-like, toward some bleak, altered reality.

"Think of them as an alignment of terrestrial wormholes," he elaborated, "and that with each passage, space-time winnows in some fractional, imperceptible way"—all this, of course, spoken from a state of herbal intoxication, yet lucid enough in that moment and in memory that I catch myself glancing at the empty seat beside me. I urged him at the time to say more, though not from as elevated a plane as he and certainly while in possession of the steering wheel. His improvisation, or at least the part of it that still vexes: "… leading us, in the end, to a dark, obliterative warp of acceleration; of passing through. And then we're there. We've arrived. The antimatter is redolent of a deep fryer."

"Arrived where?" I felt more than justified in asking. "And wait—wouldn't it have already happened? You know, 'A Billion Burgers Served' and all that?"

"Maybe it has," he said with his shiny-toothed smile, though notably he wasn't dead yet, as he is now, and could afford to be casual about vast unknowns.

As I leave the last of Redding behind, Brooke's name appears on the display. I fish for the nuts Renata packed and maintain my speed.

A flicker of lights in the concession area prompts a synchronized raising of half-emptied wine cups. I navigate through the crowd, massaging my ear along the way. I've read that prolonged close contact with electromagnetic devices can affect mortality, but it's worth wondering if they've controlled for scorching reprimands over grave failings in judgment that are occasionally transmitted through them.

"Bad?" Daniel asks, allowing a respectful interval to pass.

"Not great," I tell him, still somewhat in the mode of choosing my words carefully.

He nods sagely, blows a raspberry, then dips into the slender canon of male empathy—"Yeah, you had to expect that"—and it is somehow strangely consoling.

We tend to our beers awhile, and then I say, if only to consolidate Brooke's words into memory, "One of the things she pointed out … she said, 'He's been gone for more than twenty years. You've never met him. You don't know him or anything about him. And you just left your two-year-old child there. Without asking me.'"

"Wow, that's a little harsh. Not harsh—clarifying."

"Clarifying, yes."

"Not totally unreasonable, though. Not indiscriminate."

"She also said, along the same basic lines—she said this a few times—'You didn't tell me. You didn't tell me he was there.'"

"Yeah, but—you couldn't have done one and not the other. Asked her and not told her. And her mother had to tell her. Anyone gets that."

"Alright, well, she hasn't exactly made it there yet. In terms of seeing all the angles."

The general drift back into the amphitheater continues. We shuffle in place. I say to my brother what only moments ago I failed to say to my wife, "You know, I wouldn't have left Simon there. I wouldn't. But hell, I trust Renata. I totally trust her. Brooke wants that, right? She would have said something, not allowed me to leave, whatever …"

"You don't have to tell me."

"And he seemed, I don't know—not too bad off. A little compromised, maybe. In an old-hippie kind of way. Not a menace, though. Nothing even close to that."

"And he's his grandfather!"

"That's right! Although, yeah … probably not something I can point out."

There is a final, admonitory dimming of the lights, and we head back to our seats. The evening is cooler now, but dry and still, and I don't at all regret being here and having my mind engaged. It's odd to think Brooke would approve, if only the circumstances were different. She has often tugged me along to the ballet, and to interpretive dance as well, and I have come to an appreciation of both.

The second half of the performance resolves in a scene with the dancers arranged in such a way as to suggest the trees and undergrowth of a dwarf forest. Two sprites, one of whom is Claire, slither and prowl amid the rustling arms and hands. It is the best view we've had of her this evening, and I am struck anew by her wild, flame-red hair and her peaked forehead, which has crept up in the years I have known her from an already tenuous height. The visual effect of the piece is clever and pleasing and redeems somewhat the hyperactivity of the work before intermission.

The curtain call is a drawn-out affair, which is often the way of things with high art. Daniel and I loiter in place while the aisles clear, then make our way backstage. The space in which we find Claire and the rest of the troupe recalls others I've seen in lower-rung venues: tattered walls and plank floors, sparse lighting, exposed pipes in the slow act of shedding their insulation. Props and mounds of costumes lie everywhere, and some of the dancers, the males in particular, are still visibly perspiring. Any adornments worn during the last piece, save for leotards, have been shed or partially shed, and assorted outer garments are being pulled on. It hardly seems necessary, but several of the cast and crew have scarves on, large and loose around the neck. The outré, painted ghoulishness of the audience is intensified in here, as others who are granted access crowd in. Daniel, being Daniel, comfortable anywhere in any situation, isn't fazed by all this, but I feel acutely out of place in my jeans and cotton jersey.

After an elaborate social pollination of the room, Claire greets me with a vanishing smile, then embraces me in a maneuver almost entirely devoid of physical contact … which suits me, of course, but it's as if she has me inside a classic first-position arabesque. She endures my plaudits with a restraint that causes me to go a little too far with them, but Daniel looks uncomplicatedly happy with our interaction. It comes as a surprise, then, in the wake of an exchange I am not a part of and fail to entirely track, when Claire separates from us in a manner that suggests we won't see her tonight once things break up here, which is already in progress, clearly. Daniel says something about her schedule, about there being "two shows tomorrow and one the next day," so with walk-throughs, performances, and downtime, apparently, she can't exactly hit the bars with us. Of course she can't, and I wouldn't have expected her to, but I am staggered by this all the same—not for myself but for my brother. The general plan, I assumed, was that Daniel and I would explore the area during the day—Crater Lake, for sure, and possibly the caves or a float on the Rogue—and the three of us would convene after the evening program, at least for a quiet hour or two. I anticipated also some impromptu time on my own, naturally. Yet Daniel doesn't seem especially put out by this, so I must not have the full picture.

We exit to an unlit Jacksonville side street and begin to gather our bearings, but I can't quite leave the matter alone. Daniel takes in my restatement of the facts as they appear, then says, "Right, there's that, plus we broke up last night for the hundredth time."

"What? Here? You fly three thousand miles to see her dance and you split up?"

"Better here than that horrible, depressing, rat-defiled city she lives in," he says with a kind of screwball defiance I recognize almost from toddlerhood. "Besides, it's more like … we're just going to let things die down for a while. She knew you were coming, so that made it easier, I think."

"All right, so that's perfect. Because I'm always trying to make things easier. You know, so relationships I'm not involved in can 'die down,' for example."

"I've always looked up to you for that."

"Daniel, you weren't supposed to riff on that. This is serious, isn't it?"

"Not really, no. I was pretty sure it was going to happen. I still made the trip. Anyway, it's probably just until her contract doesn't get renewed and she moves back. Or, if it does, until—I don't know—never."

"Sounds like you can live with it either way."

"Nah, only that I'll worry about it when I have to," he says, and I realize that's as far as he'll go toward acknowledging any amount of concern. I reflect on how with Brooke and me, never mind prior relationships, there were countless touch-and-go landings, and how none of them were like this—so completely absent of nervous grief. Not that I buy the entire "Hell if I care" attitude, necessarily. Yet the next words out of his mouth are "I'm going to faint if I don't eat," something I have actually seen him do and a reinforcement both of his weighting of the present circumstances and of my own stabbing hunger.

We opt for the short drive back to Medford. Our hotel is there and has the advantage of sharing its parking lot with an alehouse. Though it mostly goes undiscussed, having only to stumble back to our room in a few hours lessens the probability of heaping one regrettable situation on top of another—something, from experience, we're both wary of.

The inside of the pub is immediately familiar for its aura of transience and lack of local flavor. An aspect of being supported entirely by budget lodgings, amid which it sits, hovers under every faded, game fowl themed lamp-shade. There are, I am aware, having explored the area with Brooke, any number of wonderful establishments a short distance away. But spending time to search one out seems superfluous at the moment—because, of course, Brooke isn't here to insist; because Daniel wouldn't care; and, again, because we're both dizzy with hunger.

Gazing at the menu, I become quantifiably aware of my mind detaching from reason, an involuntary response Renata has counseled me to become mindful of. "Close your eyes, center your breathing, attain *dharmata*, then look again," she says, and I have, in fact, found it surprisingly helpful in arriving at smarter decisions, even if I some-times regret it when the platters arrive. This has enraged Brooke, though she endures it better now than when she first connected it to Renata's Zen evangelism.

"Hey, don't fall asleep on me," Daniel says, but I am confidently past the siren call of fish and chips, burgers, and the like, and can laugh off the remark.

We order when the server returns with our porters, and it feels as though the evening, the entire weekend, is starting anew. Something about a cold glass, a creamy head, a lacquered table, and a few wide-open days and nights to knock around with a little brother you haven't seen in a couple of years.

"So, what's the plan?" he asks, wearing well and enviably his newly acquired air of freedom.

We were still marginally in possession of ourselves last night when Daniel, hearing me go on about Lonny, strung together certain elements of his reappearance—absentmindedly at first and then with a kind of match-lit inspiration. Acreage. Humboldt County. The hazy, weather-beaten, lone-wolf demeanor. Even the vintage El Camino, which I don't necessarily get, but which Daniel, a connoisseur of old Chevys, spun into the iconic, free-booting, outlaw-from-the-hills conveyance.

Beyond the jolt of recognition, I winced at the thought of having to tell Brooke. Open minded in most ways, she holds a deep aversion to recreational drugs. The news would injure her. *Or has she known all along and kept it from me? Is that where the aversion came from?* Those questions arrived an instant later.

"Jeff, go back," Daniel says, coming out of what I thought was a dead sleep.

"Back where?" I ask, glancing at the mirror. I've just taken a hard curve and can see only green behind us.

"To the—the statuary place. We just passed it."

I find a safe turnout a mile or so down the road and swing around. A narrow clearing soon comes into view encompassing a shack, a small parking area, and a regiment of anthropomorphic wood sculptures standing guard. We pull in next to a decrepit orange camper, its rusted rims sunk into the ground. Directly in front of us looms a painted scaffold of shorn tree limbs crowned with jade eyes, burl tongue, and lathed, foot-long incisors—the type of creature that, were it alive, would dance in circles as we lay lashed to a pyre.

Daniel murmurs, "So I did actually see this. I wasn't sure."

"I can understand wanting to clear that up," I say, taking in not only the sight in front of us but the smaller, equally bizarre totems positioned around it. I do, in fact, recognize this place: one of those curious roadside attractions you take note of the first time, less so the second, then fail to observe in any individualized sense thereafter. A static detail on the edge of the canvas. I'd never have stopped if not for Daniel.

We step out for a closer look. The dirt lot is knotted with conifer roots and padded with needles. An assortment of gnomes, woodland creatures, and mythic beasts stand about in no identifiable order. The bladework and joinery appear surprisingly intricate and defy the tawdriness of the overall spectacle.

The shack, or shop, is set back against the trees, past two forlorn metal gateposts. Inside, we find a braced length of raw timber arranged with carvings—some, miniaturized variations of the figures outside; others ranging from the practical to the abstract. A mantel clock. A fiddle bow. A ziggurat of sorts. Some type of helical mollusk that may or may not exist in nature. All finely shaped and finished. We are alone in the shop, but it doesn't necessarily seem like we shouldn't be here. A note on the counter apologizes for the absence and requests the honor system for payment.

I pick up a book-sized wedge with handprints routed into either side. Its tag reads "Healing Block," and the intent, according to the artist's citation, is to set one's hands prayer-like into the impressions and "draw resilience from the wood xylem." Naturally I think of Renata and contemplate making a gift of this to her. She doesn't give herself over to just anything, but the things she'll take up are often more suspect than those she'll leave alone.

Daniel drifts over, eyes down, examining a guitar slide. A bead of light skims over its polished fascia, then dissipates inside the muted cabin. "I thought you were done with all that," I say.

"Yeah, I am," he says, "or I have been. Maybe that's why Claire is kind of over me." And as casual as the remark comes off, and as elusive as the truth in such matters can often be, this isn't too different from what I've already had in mind. Sure, she was along for the ride during the years he was in bands, when he was playing all over the tristate; when there was a chance he would break through in a way that she might not. But now that he's moved on, hmm, the sales manager thing, that doesn't really fit, does it, what with her contract and New York and the scene she is immersed in there.

We drop our cash into a slot box on the wall—I decide "yes for now" on the Healing Block—and head outside. Before we get into the car, Daniel says, "You know what this is?"

"A rail slide."

"No, no. I'm asking about the trip. What this trip is."

I flash back again to last night and immediately have to suppress the beery acid in the back of my throat. Reaching through the window for my water bottle, I say, "You mean besides incredibly stupid and not at all thought through?"

"Right. Besides that."

"I give up. What?"

"It's a pilgrimage. We're on this … journey. To see this tumbledown, beatnik farmer. Who was taken for dead. Who's been out in the wilds, living off the grid, cultivating his plants, hoarding his capital. Possibly going faint in the head. Oblivious to the world—to the wife and daughter—he left behind. We're seeking answers. Claiming your son's birthright. It feels epic. Seriously, to me it feels that way. I've always wanted to do something like this."

I digest this for a minute. I look closely at Daniel, whose chain-pulling is almost indistinguishable from his standard way of communicating. Traffic wheels by a few yards from where we stand. The road and clearing are raked by tall shadows. A seed cone plinks the roof of the car, directly between us.

"Daniel," I start in after a long, unsatisfying pull of warm water. "You know, that would be pretty funny. It really would. But Brooke, she's not exactly happy with me right now. She's ignoring my calls. She is, if I know her at all, seriously questioning her life choices, which she does a lot of these days—specifically those that involve me … which, if we're being honest, given your own situation with Claire, would make this trip, this *journey*, extremely pathetic. Beyond pathetic. A loser and loser kind of thing. So … so, it's not really funny then, is it? Or maybe it's so fucking funny I can't laugh. But there may not be a distinction."

"Jeff, all I was saying—"

"And we're not seeking anything. Or claiming anything. This is about … it's about … I don't know what it's about. But if I can tell Brooke—if there is a chance I can tell Brooke, 'He's growing corn up there, or gourds, or African violets, or none of those, he's a shepherd, or a poet, but no, he didn't drop out of your life for twenty-plus years to grow weed,' then, then … I'll tell you what: we should be on our way to Crater Lake right now. Forget that, we should be there already. Because, you know, that's *epic*; that's amazing. It's amazing and shocking, and what we're doing, where we're going … well, it's not really in the same category."

Daniel, who has a congenital immunity to taking anything personally, especially from me, says, "I'm pretty sure that's not corn country down there." He says this having arched his back and oriented himself southward, as if he were hitching around in his saddle.

Don't respond, I tell myself, *just don't*, and I step away to check for messages and to see again if I can reach Brooke. Of course, we are in a stand of giant evergreens that extends for miles in every direction, so nothing goes through, and I am tempted to ask my brother if he has another observation on the natural world he'd like to contribute. But no, no, the conversation is over. We're going where we're going, even if the impetus behind it feels so much less urgent now than it felt last night. And who knows, maybe we'll blow through Humboldt, go fetch Simon, and head on into the city. And what was that, anyway, about Simon's birthright? I don't want anything to do with the guy's land, and Brooke certainly wouldn't, even if we are doomed to be lifetime renters on the most expensive spit of real estate on earth.

Back out on the road, I figure if Daniel is so keen on what we're doing, then it's a whiplash response to the breakup with Claire, and he's only searching for somewhere to focus his mind a while. It galls me to think this started with Claire, and I should probably let go of my issues with that woman, but they are age-old and undoubtedly returned with conviction. It is true that I always have in a sense objectified her, but not so differently than I might a nude in portraiture. She is astonishing to look at, arguably beautiful but inarguably astonishing, and she entrances in performance—which is a crucial point, *she is performing, always*, in her movements, her gestures, her social interactions. And maybe at the root of our problems is my reflexive appraisal of this, of her, which I haven't been able to stop, even at the risk of being called out. Women are often attuned to such scrutiny, of course, but the skill can't be perfect, especially where the distinctions are fine—say, between depravity and art appreciation. And if the one can't be distinguished from the other, then we find ourselves where we are, don't we? Mutual distrust, pretense, air kisses, immaculate hugs, and acute wariness where the shared object of our affection— or, in her case, now disaffection—is concerned. And I am feeling so goddam vindicated right now, unfortunately.

That particular object has closed his eyes again, I see. I don't mind, although I could use an hour myself. But he drank double what I did last night, so it's probably not going to happen.

Eventually we cross the border and roll into Crescent City, where the whiff of civilization and the possibility of a meal brings him around. After gassing up, we stop at one of those breakfast-all-day type of restaurants where, in fact, we both do order breakfast, though the actual day is nearly gone. Our omelets arrive scalloped with pan grease and seemingly banked onto the plates with a snow shovel, neither of which keeps us from the task at hand, as this is our first real nourishment since last night. *Dharmata* not attained.

While awaiting the check, I try again to reach Brooke, and this time I have all the signal I need, and again she doesn't answer. I know from speaking to Renata and Simon this morning that she is still in L.A. and that Lonny is long gone—perhaps sprucing things up for visitors, which he might have decided to count on despite my demurrals.

Jumped up on caffeine, Daniel takes the wheel, though I am wide awake now too. Ten or so miles south of town we are drawn to a stop by a large, milling herd of elk in a vast meadow on the west side of the highway. A gravel road runs along the north boundary of the meadow, so we ease down that road having a long, silent look. We reach a fork that separates to a parking lot on the right and a still narrower track that continues ahead and curves out of sight. We step outside there and watch awhile from the split-rail. Daniel says archly, "Real fauna, no choreography," and it leaves me with an unexpected twinge of relief. It's good he'll have a keepsake of sorts from this trip, one that doesn't involve the flameout with Claire.

We become aware, in the murmuring quiet, of activity behind us: a park ranger locking up a utility shed, the construction of which appears recent and perhaps not even complete. My eyes travel from the shed to a map shelter beyond it, also new, and to a towering backdrop of what must be coastal redwoods that walls off our view to the horizon.

In the time it takes for us to absorb this scene, the ranger comes up beside us. She gestures toward the open field and says, "There's a good number of them today," guiding our attention for a moment back to the elk. "If you follow the line of the creek, you'll see several cows with calves towing along behind them. They've only rejoined the herd in the last week or so."

We do as instructed, but, as we're without binoculars, the only thing that verifiably stands out amid the tall grasses and bobbing heads and shoulders are bulls with their elaborate combat apparatus.

I turn back to the ranger and am filled at a glance with a kind of raw, vestigial longing. She is in full Park Service regalia, and slack tangles of auburn hair fall carelessly from her sharp, flat-brimmed field hat. Her eyes, dark and slender, wick upward at the corners and together with her tranquil smile convey an air of savvy observation. Given the right circumstances, it must be a short conjectural leap from stewardess of nature to sylvan nymph, because I am already there … though perhaps my perspective is heightened by the spectacle of Claire's willowy interpretation last night. Brooke, too, has always looked her most irresistible to me on a foggy trail.

"So, they're always here, then?" Daniel asks.

"Oh, no. They roam along the north coast, mostly near the redwoods. Even along the beach sometimes."

"Elk on the beach …"

"Usually as a shortcut to one of their grazing areas."

She pauses there, lets linger the suggestion of untapped knowledge if only we'd ask. Daniel seems lost in thought, and my mind, too, is wandering down other tracks: one, admittedly, that leads nowhere—the same nowhere that suffocates most passing attractions; the other, a less unlikely proposition. It is in this vein that I ask about the parking lot and outbuildings. She explains that the "Service" has cut a new trail through this grove, one it aims to open to the public in the next month or so. "It's a short loop, less than five miles in all," she says. "But it's an impressive walk in the woods. Royalty the whole way through."

"Are we allowed in before then?" I inquire in that tone reserved for figures of authority who also happen to be magnificent looking. Distractions aside, a plunge into the redwoods would absolutely compensate for the miss on Crater Lake.

She turns away, scoffs quietly. Her neck attenuates in profile. "We can't stop you," she says, "or any of the others who have gone over the tape. We don't have the budget. Just try to be out before nightfall, okay?"

I have to resist chasing after her as she strides off toward her truck. It feels unjust, her lumping us in with "the others," but I suppose we had it coming.

Daniel says, "We're going on a hike?"

"Not just a hike," I tell him without bothering to elaborate. His first time in the redwoods—what is there to say?

After zipping the car into the parking lot, we fill our water bottles from a tap near the trailhead and take off almost running. Ten minutes later we're gazing up at a two-hundred-foot canopy, the early evening light ripping through in soaring, mote-filled shafts. The understory is dense with ferns and sorrel, while tanoak seedlings crane above for openings.

A mile or so in, we come to an iron bridge that traverses a small cascade. Thick snags of rhododendron crowd the near banks, along with another less-ostentatious wild-flower, these on bare, foot-high stalks with a flare of heart-shaped leaves and a white rosette preening at the very top. The echoing from the highway goes quiet here, beside the falling water, and any urgency we felt while dashing in ebbs away with the change. Listening, look-ing around, breathing everything in … it shouldn't be necessary, but I find myself making an effort to fully let go, as Daniel so obviously has. We both have our issues right now, but we are speeding away from his, coming closer to mine. Closer not only in miles but in context.

It is far too easy at the moment, in this surreal setting, and being conscious of where we're headed, to imagine some critical point of decision from long, long ago: the decision to strike personal obligations out of your mind, the people they're owed to, the life built around them … so you can surrender to the isolation; lose yourself inside of it; have it dwell inside of you. Still, it's one thing to envision the escape, to come under its thrall, and another not to ultimately repudiate it.

When we do get going again, a series of switchbacks and contours leads us out of the gulch and up to a benchland. From here the trees become almost mythically immense and often have great, jagged scars on their flanks, the signatures of ancient encounters with thunderbolt and flame.

We slow-walk the descent, and it is well into dusk before we crawl out of the creaking, spectral interior. The feeling I have, and which I assume Daniel has, is a kind of grief over exiting the realm; fear that what we've experienced isn't real, repeatable. Possibly for this reason, we decide against the drive to Eureka, the next town south of any size, and begin the search for a nearby campsite to spend the night. This leads us, quite a while later, to a sheltered melon slice of state-owned beach, having been turned away at three different area campgrounds.

As we drop down from the overlook with our gear, such as it is, we meet a group of Spaniards headed in the opposite direction. They were given the same coordinates by the same private operator we last visited, but they've decided to move on. We are not especially put out by this. The camaraderie of imperfect circumstances aside, having the beach to ourselves sounds about right at the moment. We are elated, in any event, to discover their still smoldering fire and quickly set about reviving it.

The two of us talk well into the night, though hardly at all about the big trees—maybe out of concern it would demystify the experience, if that were somehow possible. In time, we do come around to the levitation question, as certain daring souls are known to climb redwoods: tree squatters, alpinists, botanists doing research in the crowns.

Daniel tells me, "Once, when I was out with one of Dad's crews—this was after you left, J—we were running power out to a treehouse. The fire department made us hire a guy to go up and clear out the dead growth. He used a slingshot to fire up a weighted rope and lashed it down on the other side. Then he goes up the free end using a ratchet of some kind … really, really cool. I would've gone up myself if he'd have let me."

"I'm trying to imagine the slingshot you'd need for a millennial redwood."

"Yeah, maybe a grenade launcher would work. And some oxygen for the ride up."

I poke at the embers awhile, putting off the question Daniel has now made inevitable. A squall of smoke and ash floats up into the cooling air. The tide, barely illuminated, traces a skittering line between the rock piles. When I am ready, I ask, "So, how's he holding up, anyway?"

"Dad? He's bored. Working on a hundred little shit projects, not finishing anything. Alone with his rage most of the time now that Mom is gone, the business is gone, you're out here, I'm … wherever."

"That sounds about right."

"Are you guys talking? He rarely mentions it."

"Not often. He's curious about Simon, that's the main theme."

"Actually, he does go on about that. The idea of there being a 'stemwinder,' as he puts it. A male to carry on the family line. It seems important to him."

"Maybe Lonny has come around for the same reason."

"You'd think a daughter would be enough. I mean, what—twenty years, is that what you said?"

"He took off when she was Simon's age. Showed up once, for a single day, when she was eight or so. Then gone again. So twenty-five years since that day? No letters, no contact. Nothing."

"We didn't exactly have that problem, did we? No contact?"

"No. No we didn't … which, you know, looking at Brooke's situation, it's interesting. Her father was non-existent, or a kind of abstraction. Ours, he was there, all the time, the whole way through. We couldn't get the hell away from him. Just that you and I made it out with our heads attached—it's amazing to me sometimes."

"He's old and pathetic now."

"Daniel, that is in no way a comfort. In fact, it's almost an affront, now that we can do something about it."

"All right, all right, but—the one who's there, who fucks with your mind and smacks you around, versus the one who's not there, who bolts before you know him and never shows an interest. Would you make the trade?"

"Would I trade with Brooke?"

"It's rhetorical, you're not supposed to answer," he says with a laugh, which may also be a yawn, then seems to hit on something that makes him feel a little triumphant.

"Anyway, brother, we'll get to the end of all this tomorrow, won't we?"

Over the next several minutes, the fire and our desire to stay awake arrive at some equal point of diminishment. We unfurl the tarp I keep stashed with the mini-spare, then roll out our sleeping bags: one I brought along in the event some conjugal requirement forced me out of the hotel room in Medford, and Simon's, which, of course, should be in Tiburon. It is at this moment we realize Daniel will have to choose which half of his body to keep warm overnight.

While I am wriggling into my sack, my phone rings. I see that it's Brooke and huddle down to stifle the noise of the surf, mild as it is. I take a breath and prepare for whatever, having no idea where she's calling from, whether or not she has talked to Lonny, if she is still ripped at me. But she is sobbing, quietly. She says, "Jeffrey, my mother, if she doesn't take her pills … her cancer, um," and that's all that comes, and that's all that's going to come. And while I have to refocus and the subject isn't a pleasant one, I am grateful to have the chance to console her. To inch back toward level ground.

Daniel tugs on my sleeve and says, "Jeff, look. She wasn't kidding."

He points toward the tree line, where several bull elk, maybe ten or so, move north to south in slow, silent procession. Mist lifts calmly off the water, seeps into the woods.

Brooke appears farther up the beach, sees what we see. She takes off her cap and shakes out her hair, which is longer than it has been in years. She says, "It's a bachelor herd, exiled by the other males. They roam along the coast and feed on shore grasses."

I am ecstatic to see her and call out, "Brooke, you don't need to worry. I've bought something for Renata that will help her get better."

She gazes at me doubtfully and says, "Jeffrey, that's kind of you. But my mother is already dead. Didn't you know?"

I turn back to Daniel and am about to ask if he's cold. But Claire is lounging next to him, Simon's kiddie bag wound sinuously around her neck.

She silences me with her eyes.

Maybe a quarter of an hour has passed since we caught sight of the El Camino under a canvas shelter and eased in near to it. Other makeshift structures dot the clearing, including a small pole barn that appears to double as a residence. The barn, or house, is a patchwork affair, and its washboard roof bears evidence of fearsome storm damage.

There has been no sign of anyone—any person—inside or outside. Of the two brindle-striped hounds that lunged at our still-moving car, one has gone film-eyed and tipped over into an exhausted pile; the other, which isn't fully visible right now, seems to have gained purchase on the sidewall of the rear passenger-side tire or the fender just above.

Daniel says, "Uh, maybe you should set the brake," which I immediately do, but the only noticeable effect is to bring a certain coherence to the shudder of the unibody.

Perhaps cueing off the frenzy of the dogs, vultures have begun circling overhead. The sight of this gives rise to unsettling thoughts, and I miss the irony at first when

Daniel breaks in again and says, "One of us could run out, create a distraction. You're older."

"What about trip wires? Snares? Guys up here do crazy shit to protect their plants."

"Hey, now that you mention it, I don't actually see anything. I mean, not that we would, out here in the open. But it just looks like the usual, scruffy, backwoods stake you'd find anywhere."

As we're peering around, looking for corroboration we know we won't find, Lonny slips into view at the far edge of the tree cut and stops there. He is dressed in camouflage and has on the same gnawed leather hat as in Tiburon. His face is smudged with grease paint or something similar, and three monstrous arrows stick up behind his back, presumably from a suitably large quiver.

Daniel says under his breath, "What the fuck," a sentiment I would almost certainly share if not for my one prior exposure to him two days before. It occurs to me that the car has stopped shaking and the brindles have disappeared, though it isn't clear where they've gone.

In the seconds that follow, Lonny collects himself and begins to lope in our direction. We step slowly out of the car so as to make ourselves identifiable, all the while trying to ascertain the whereabouts of the dogs. Upon reaching us, Lonny studies Daniel as if his presence defies all accountability.

"The sisters told me there were two of you," he eventually says, which surprises me at first, but then he taps a transceiver clipped to his belt by way of explanation. We had, in fact, sought directions from a woman raking out a swale a quarter mile or so up the road, near a sign that read "Lost Hills Abbey for Sisters of the Nazarene." Apparently they are in ready contact.

Rising just above the insect chatter, Daniel leans in and says, "I'm Dan, the little brother—we're practically family," and I can only swallow my horror at his complete lack of boundaries. Lonny stares at him, blankly, at first, and then with a kind of scholarly recognition.

"Looks like we pulled you away from something," I say, hoping to reel things back to an agreeable starting point.

He gestures vaguely in the direction of the abbey and says, "They … the sisters, they're having a certain pestilence issue over there."

"For which you need—" I begin to ask, at which point he lets his sling fall to the ground, and I notice that one of the arrows has some sort of launching mechanism affixed to it, and all three have winged steel blades in place of ordinary bullet tips. They might not be arrows at all.

Surely having caught my drift, he reaches down and unclamps the launcher from the shaft, then raises it with a flourish. He runs his palm over the wood grain and says, "It's an atlatl. In terms more germane to the Anthropocene, a spear thrower. Properly weighted and balanced, those darts release at a hundred miles per hour. They can take down a mastodon."

"I'm guessing the problem isn't that serious," Daniel says.

Lonny, offering no indication he's heard, continues through his paces: recradling the projectile, leveling it above his shoulder, then extending his free arm along the same axis. Allowing for his getup, it is an archetypal cave-wall pose and summons at once both the specter of the melee and the conceit of the hominid—the sheer magic of being able to recoil and hurl. And as it gels in my mind that he is about to take this to its ritualistic end, he does so, gunning his arm forward, then snapping off the shot. A brisk, low "woof" ricochets through the air, and Daniel and I both leave the ground … remembering, of course, the hounds, though the sound clearly wasn't theirs. A warm, fluttering silence lingers in its aftermath.

"Where did it go?" Daniel asks.

Lonny peers intently toward the woods as if awaiting a return volley. "We'll find it later," he says warily. "Now, what was it we were talking about?"

"The nuns," I say, taking several seconds to pick up the thread. "You were telling us about the nuns. You're working for them, helping them out—is that it?"

"Now and again. They're self-reliant to an extreme most men could never contemplate."

"Sure, sure, but the spear thing—"

"Atlatl. Adapted for barrage warfare by the Aztecs. Also, a highly effective, non-incendiary culling weapon against wild boar, provided you stay downwind and understand how to make an approach. Without a scent, they can't tell a horse from a hockey stick."

"What … what are you saying?"

"*Sus scrofa.* Wild hog. There are more feral hogs in these parts than bear, cougar, and coyote combined. And they'll tear up anything their guts tell them to. Which is every-thing. And for the last three nights they've been laying waste to the summer harvest over at the abbey—crops the sisters live on and barter."

"So, you're wrangling pigs," Daniel says. "Of course you are. Why didn't we get that straight off?"

"This animal shares very little in its capacity for mayhem with the domesticated pig."

"Lonny," I hear myself say, addressing him in the famil-iar for the first time and immediately wishing I hadn't.

"The nuns—*the nuns*—want you to kill the hog? Or hogs? With spears that travel a hundred miles per hour?"

"Killing they will not themselves do. Bait hoppers and firearms they don't condone."

Daniel moves off a few paces, lowers his hands to his knees. He gazes awhile at the parched weeds. The thought flits through my mind that he might be hungry, but we stopped for coffee in Arcata and I am certain he ate something there.

Without prompting, Lonny says abstractly, and seemingly more to the spirits than to us, "If it were only the damn vegetables they were ravaging around here, we could almost come to an understanding."

The words … the conceptualization of those words … fills the expanse from where we stand to every visible thing. This takes a second. It takes no time. The realization, the fully decorated panorama, is carved into the light and left there to admire. *Of course you're wrangling pigs. Of course the pigs are high, gorged on psychoactive pulp. Rapture is often attendant to the spilling of blood. Why must the slaughterer alone lay claim to it?*

There is an abrupt, convulsive sound, and it belongs to Daniel. He tenses and shudders. When he straightens up, his gaze is a medium of pure, airless hilarity. We commiserate. We eye one another through the cynosure of shared memory. Every prior absurdity in our lives has come in service of this absurdity. Casting around, there appears no navigable way back from this moment to any serious discussion about Lonny's rejection of Brooke, nor what he's after now, if anything.

I think back to last night, to the swap Daniel had conceived: the wrathful father for the phantom father. My dramatist friend, he of the "terrestrial wormholes," in his last piece—never to my knowledge staged but shown to me in snatches while being written—in this piece there was a line, one I have never quite shaken free of: "The miseries of our childhood are indispensable to us." It seems laughable on its face, but in context it read as an avowal of ownership rather than woe, and ownership in that sense is primal; devotional. Brooke and I would never have done the deal. Wouldn't do it still. We are wedded to our stories even more so than to each other. That they've become intertwined hasn't changed this, though it does allow either of us to influence the narrative of the other going forward. Such is the pretext, then, for what Brooke will ultimately learn, and not learn, of this encounter. As for my friend, well … he very soon thereafter went to the trouble of killing himself. As if to rejoin the argument: *as we are indispensable to them.*

When I check back in on my surroundings, Lonny and Daniel are standing side by side in muted conference. Lonny, grasping one of the arrows, is sketching coordinates in the dirt: his property, the abbey, adjacent public lands; streams and wildlife corridors; areas where he has found wallows and fresh scat, recently furrowed vegetation.

Dusk is a few hours off. We could, if we leave soon, make it to Tiburon before Simon's bedtime. I would have to twist Daniel's arm, I can see, and it might be unreasonable for me to insist. After all, there is something about this scenario that beckons, that carries the scent of the long course of time: a tribal hunt, consecrated by virgins, and made intimate by the thrust of the pike.

Lonny says, apropos of nothing Daniel has asked, "The parasite load on these creatures is alarming."

"Undoubtedly that's true," Daniel replies authoritatively, as though he has cracked the code of Lonny's random asides.

I retreat to the car for a drink of water. When I turn back around, Lonny is letting himself into his residence. Daniel has picked up the spear thrower and is studying its design. He drags his thumb slowly, attentively, along the mounting surface; puzzles over a small stone spindle at its midsection. I watch for a time, then call out to him, "Okay, so you were right. This is pretty epic."

He laughs and bobs his head, all the while trying to seat one of the arrows.

"Jeff," he says, "I just want to say thank you, *thank you*," and I know he's not referring to my mea culpa but to a higher-level consideration: that being here is worth every bit of having broken up with Claire, for however long that lasts, anyway.

He continues to tinker, tries to find a stance that feels natural; eventually trains his free arm toward some arbitrary target in the manner that Lonny had done. It is at this moment that the two purebreds reappear, screaming around the far side of the barn in pursuit of a rabbit. One of them stays hot after the rabbit, but the other, having spotted us, alters its trajectory without breaking stride.

Daniel doesn't have the best history with canines, but he remains calm, the dog squarely in his sights. Of course, Lonny then gallops into view, several yards behind, moving high and fine along the same path, *old track star that he is*. He is bellowing at the top of his lungs, though his words are lost to the exigencies of the immediate present.

Daniel flicks his gaze toward me, dazzled by the possibilities. With a deference he has been saving just for this moment, and leaving no room to second guess, he mouths the appeal, "Jeff, what should I do?"

SURFACE TO AIR

A courier is testing delivery by aerial drone in a several-square-block area near the house I am rehabbing, so it draws my attention but doesn't throw me when the now familiar black hexapod appears with a shipping box in its talons. It is midafternoon and all but one of the siders have left for the day. They've skinned most of the east wall, uncovering a dark vein of wood rot along its base: only the latest of the many unpleasant surprises I've had since acquiring this place out of pre-foreclosure.

There is a rhythmic chirping sound as the craft approaches, akin to sawing insects. The workman peers out from the shadows beneath the eaves, shields the glare with his free hand. I watch him closely because, honestly, that's the more interesting aspect now, to see the reaction. I catch his eye after it's gone, after he has gazed at the empty sky for a while, and there it is: the look that says, yeah, I've heard about this, and now I've seen it, everything will be a little different now, won't it?

Sometimes I agree and sometimes I wonder. Will people really accept having their homes buzzed by low-flying robots, with concealed payloads, able to surveil or rain hailfire or make off with as much as they leave behind? Even if it is for the purpose of airlifting more crap into their lives? My son, who, at fifteen, owns discerning views on such matters, along with a deep grounding in the speculative arts, assures me it is a transition technology, before subsurface freight-hyperloops; before, ultimately, the proliferation of four-dimensional, mixed-material printing, making quaint the entire notion of needing anything delivered but raw, combinative feedstocks. Or perhaps only their catalysts. Just add water, if it's still around.

I collect a shovel left spoon-up in the middle of the yard and plant it upright into a mound of soil. Simon, the son, having taken an interest in a depression in the lawn thirty feet or so from the foundation, began excavating here over the weekend—this, in keeping with his general policy that whatever help he'll lend me on this or any other project will be self-directed. He has made admirable progress, though not as yet to any revelatory end. A neighbor who snoops around here on occasion has alluded, variously, to an old drainage issue, an abandoned packrat midden, a stump that was pulverized and left to collapse. He's winging it, obviously, and not necessarily to be helpful. The entire block seems on edge about what I might do with this place. I am happy to tell them, *Not lose money,* which at this point appears legitimately in doubt. They should be more concerned with the drone.

"The girl asked me to give this to you," says my daughter, coming up from behind. She hands me an envelope, which I open while she hooves the loose dirt at the edge of pile. "The girl," actually a woman in her twenties, is one of the Craigslist-sourced crew to whom I've rented the hangar, a detached garage with a kind of rigging-loft and double-height rollup door situated at the far end of the property, the lot being an acre altogether.

"Hey, cut it out," I say, as she triggers a small avalanche into the hole, undoubtedly aware of whose handiwork she is undoing. "How was school?"

"Daddy, they're smoking over there," she says, with a certain borrowed nonchalance—probing for some kind of reaction, which she has always done, only now with a little more savvy.

"I hope that's the worst thing they're doing," I say.

"No, I mean, what they're smoking. They're not real cigarettes."

"I knew what you meant, and it's okay," I tell her. "It's legal now, right? At least where we live. Anyway, they'll only be there a few months, until we're ready to sell."

In fact, I don't have a complete picture of what they're up to, the girl, Perri, amidst her constellation of piercings and rag bracelets, and her mumbly, insolent friends, all just out of college or, in one or two cases, still in. A "proof-of-concept" affair, some esoteric fusion of game control and rocketry, which is enough to know for the short time it matters. The main thing, the only thing, really, is the easy, off-the-ledger cash when almost everything is flowing in the opposite direction.

I count out the bills in the envelope, a distressed assortment of ones, fives, and tens. It looks like they took up a collection, but it's all there.

"Maybe you should go over and ask them for some," Kira ventures, clearly unsatisfied with my indifference and doing well to snap me out of it.

"Have you been eavesdropping again?" I say, giving her the dad eye, while thinking back to the one or two very brief and hardly explicit conversations I've had with Brooke that would in any way relate to her insinuation.

"No, you guys just always assume we're not listening or we don't understand. You're actually terrible at keeping secrets."

"How can you be sure?" I say. "We could have a ton of secrets."

"You don't, though."

"Okay, probably not. But that can go both ways, and it just so happens that I'm on to one of yours."

"So, what is it?"

"That you're trying to sound way too grown up right now, and it's not working. Not with the double-pony and orange flip-flops."

"Dad," she sighs with an exasperated slouch, then hoists up her school backpack and veers off toward the greenbelt trail that winds through to our home a couple of blocks away. "Love you," she says without looking back and at the very edge of my radar, and I say it in return.

Maybe you should go over and ask them for some … wow, even for Kira, a little brash.

I glance over and the siding guy is gone, his extension ladder down. Just me and the object I flay myself against in all its fallen, semi-Craftsman grandeur. Today it's the deck railing, which I have been scraping and sanding for hours. Not that anyone could tell. I didn't think this would be easy, but damn, I'm a contractor's son. This is in my blood.

As it turns out, other things are there too, in my blood. Or, more precisely, in the marrow from which it seeps. Discovered about a week after we closed on the investment property. The kids know, generally. The small picture, not the big one. But they've seen when it knocks me on my back. I haven't smoked weed in ages, but, sure, I did float the idea to Brooke, and she didn't immediately swat it down. Significant, as she has some grim family history there which I am always careful to leave alone.

It's not so much for the discomfort, I don't mind saying, which is being addressed in other ways. More to settle my nerves, ratchet things down a little. Find some equilibrium from time to time. And now, unbelievably to me, I can drive a mile away and buy it over the counter, set myself up. Which, despite Kira's quick ears and lively imagination, I haven't yet done. It remains a small source of pride that I ever dropped the habit in the first place, right before Brooke came along. My life isn't so full of triumphs that I can walk away from any single one of them.

Anyway, that 'love you, love you back' routine, there was a time when I feared Kira might be growing out of that, though she's still only twelve. But she started in with it again after "the conversation," the talk you have with your kids when something like this shows up in your life. I am programmed to reciprocate.

"Can you PU Simi from XC @ 5?" reads a text from Brooke. I tell her I will, and it leaves me with a small jolt of resolve. On a project so open-ended, with such a multitude of needs, and with my energy not always at its peak right now, it helps having cutoff times, brings a certain pace to my work. Maybe Brooke has come to sense this or maybe she's juggling as usual.

I fire up the belt sander and start whaling on the rail cap. With the noise cancellers on, it's only at the last instant that I see the faint, spidery shadow glide across the deck, scale the wall, and disappear.

"How are you planning to get that out of there?" I ask.

"I will," he says, immediately drawing attention to my mistake.

I have learned—no, been taught, and rather cruelly, it feels—that questions about process are no longer worthy of a response. This can happen years before parents are ready for it, even though a future where it might be useful is easy to foresee.

"You could just leave it, you know. Backfill and cover," I say, committing a second unforced error: suggesting a course of action. Not deliberately to earn his pity, unspoken, ungestured, but implied. Though, again, that too might have its time and place.

"Okay, I'll leave you to it then," I say, filling the open frequency, then amble off to take measure of the several bundles of cedar lath that have appeared in the driveway. A tile saw shrieks at migraine pitch from an open second floor window.

Apparently, before development began creeping in, this plateau was logged, mined, and logged again. So uncovering a tire in the yard, three feet below grade—a large, ribbed tire off some gnashing piece of machinery—is not unexplainable. Nor is it without a certain pathos, connecting as it does my own practice of industry on this ground to those from other epochs. Part of me says leave the dead alone, or at least their heavy equipment. Another part says let's see what the kid can do. It's a hundred-pound tire, minimum. Triple that with the dirt caked into its bladder. And maybe there is an entire backhoe under there, like Sue beneath the exposed femur. With China driving up the price of ferrous metals, I could flip that into a loan payment, even after spiffing Simon for his labor.

I stop to inspect the new cage-wire sealing off the crawl space, nailed up while I was in town visiting my hematologist. There *were* rats here, give the neighbor credit for that. Only they were under the house, shredding the vapor barrier and insulation, gouging the subfloor. Trying to ream their way in.

My hemo is like that, a tunneler. Twice he's come at me with the bone needle and now says he needs to do it again. Imagine having a well spike driven in and your pith siphoned backward through its conduit. It is not pain, per se. More like voltage in the river channel.

"It is the only way we can tell what's going on," he assures me, then cites the exoticism of plasmacytic differentiation, points to the skyrocketing values of my free light chains.

I look back, and the boy, the young man, already my height now, only thirty pounds lighter, and I have never been stout, is no longer standing over the hole, nor is he anywhere in sight. Only the shovel, lying in its usual skull-cracking position in the middle of the lawn. As is so often the case, "I will" meant "I will at a time of my choosing."

Never mind. My heart remains full of desperate, unabashed love. Though this too is no longer worthy of a response.

Is the light free, are the chains light, or is the light in a chain … that is free … only not from itself?

How odd, the disease marker whose name subverts the combining of forms; eschews the root, the prefix, and the suffix in favor of lilt and aspiration and the well-placed note of anguish. *The tools of the poet find the hand of the clinician, lie weightless there*—or so I once read in Richard Selzer's work, or perhaps of Richard Selzer. The transaction could go the other way, I imagine, but then you are in the realm of the faith healer.

I am beading silicone into seams along the baseboard and casing. It is not a feat of skill, and there is the vague, devaluing association with Silly String. But it does require a certain care and tenderness, qualities I have gradually come into some possession of. And the actual millwork, the mitering and wrapping and joining, lies beyond, well beyond, my capabilities.

Over the sill of the dining room window, which I am working beneath, I catch sight of—rather, I imprint, for the sequence has begun and ended, and mere seconds have elapsed—a long, spear-tipped flash of white light originating from inside the hangar. The hangar lies across the meadow, and I am at an angle from its bay, so it is, or was, difficult to tell. But a contrail has appeared leading back to it, punctuated by a small detonation no more than fifty or sixty feet off the ground. A bright, short-lived particle shower gives way to a sustained final chord of clarity and stillness.

Now one of Perri's gang darts out, shirtless, breathless, a slight lad I have come to know as Kon, the sparkly-eyed, semester-abroad student from Japan. Perri and four or five of the others emerge a moment later, minus the excitability. Their launch apparently gone awry, they mime the language of youthful disgust. Ants are crushed. Unwashed hair is raked. Skinny forearms skip invisible stones.

Despite the instantaneous appeal of a conflagration that would engulf not just the hangar but the house, my mind promptly assumes the perspectives of fire marshal, insurer, and banker alike. *Residential zoning violation. Unpermitted use of accessory building. Absence of overhead flame suppression. Personal liability for grievous injury or loss. Denial of claim. Demand for debt repayment. Referral to law enforcement and tax authorities.* And on and on and catastrophically on.

Still on one knee and with a dollop of caulk on my finger, I determine on the spot to evict Perri and her ill-mannered gearheads. But then a familiar figure takes shape among them, unmistakable in its smoldering adolescence and bony patrilineage. He glances toward the house, beams an appeal through its walls and windows as though intuiting my gaze: *I've come to this on my own; please don't fuck it up for me.*

We have a conversation, Brooke and I. We discuss our shy teenager. We fret, as we so often do, over the need to break the pattern: the eternally closed bedroom door; the scant peer exposure outside of school settings; the intravenous relationship to various electronic devices; the extreme cognitive immersion in all things dystopian and futuristic; the solitary interactions with garden implement or spinner reel or pebble-grain ball against driveway backboard. A natural trail runner, Simon, he seeks spacing in the middle of the pack, as unwilling to chase the fleet boys as to let the plodders catch up.

Brooke says what I already know, "We can't throw them out, not now; not when he's found his way over there, made a connection with them. Okay, so it's not ideal. They're not his age, and they're a little, uh … hmm …"

"Feral."

"No, not that. Just sort of a misfit bunch, which makes sense, right? And they're super smart, and they've all thrown in together, and they obviously have good hearts, so …"

"They could blow up the hangar," I say, just to hear myself affirm the absurdity of letting things go on, which, again, I know I'll do.

"With him in it," I add, sans the cigar and fake mustache.

"Well, talk to them, then. Tell them not to blow up the hangar."

"I already have. Their reassurance was not reassuring."

"What did they say, exactly? Do we even know what they're doing over there at this point?"

"Our translator has gone over to the other side. We have to discount everything."

"Oh, that's probably true," she concedes, pausing to rationalize the situation, for herself and then for me—a tendency I often have trouble indulging. "Even so," she says, "we can still apply perspective to the situation, can't we? I mean, what are the odds, really, of something happening to him? Something genuinely awful? Especially now, with their little mistake already behind them. Not zero, but it's never zero."

"The potential for mortal injury, Brooke, is not confined to our son. And wait—aren't I supposed to be the one making that argument? Saying, 'Screw it, stay in the game, swing at the damn ball. A couple of heaters under the chin will be good for you.'"

"You've never done that. Or, I should say, you've never really been convincing when you have."

"Nice."

"In fact, sometimes it's quite hilarious—"

"Stop …"

"Jeffrey," she says, with her sly, man-whisperer smile, making me wait for the final payoff but telegraphing its peaceable intent. "You should consider not taking that as an insult."

We banter a bit more, and mostly I listen. It feels like a play argument. I have the sense there is an outlying truth here but can't quite navigate the terrain. I could change tactics and mention the weed use and Simon's likely exposure to it, which, for Brooke, would instantly ricochet to thoughts of her absentee father, stashed away in the hinterlands of California pot country (or, quite possibly, several feet underneath by now). Justly or not, she'd draw a line to her son for fear of some rogue intergenerational bond—a concern, in the abstract, which I share but have less standing on than perhaps even Brooke is aware. Yet, for reasons that come as a surprise to me, and that are arguably a little self-serving, I trust Simon on this … or, rather, feel the need to test my trust in him, *our trust* in him; to validate fifteen years of mindful parenting; to see if anything we have ever said or done matters one single iota. So I keep my mouth shut on the topic and gamble that Kira will as well.

It is outlandish, I know, to conflate the two risks: an unstable cocktail of flammable propellants and a mildly elevating cultivar. Having to account for the lesser of those perils in the face of the other defies all credulity. All the more reason to leave the worms safely in the can, so to speak.

"By the way, we received this in the mail today," Brooke says, then hands me a letter from the county stating that the present configuration of the septic system is in violation of code: a requiem, of a sort, for my last hope of profit on the deal and likely a multi-month delay in permitting for occupancy. "Maybe you should go lie down," she says.

Gresso, the septic guy, rambles on good-naturedly about his sons' reluctance to take up his profession, an aversion that hardly needs explaining. I listen, because at any time he might slip in an actual number I can place on dropping in new pump housings and reengineering the drain field, but my eyes lie on a gray, misshapen tire suspended from the hulking bigleaf maple on the near side of the hangar.

The tire. Maybe I've noticed its absence and maybe I haven't, though generally there has been too much else to bother with. But, all right, a tire swing. Not Nerf guns, not stress balls, not ping pong or air hockey; not yoga mats or a massage chair. A tire swing. Old school. So a little respect is in order.

While Gresso continues to yak and my prospective costs continue to rise, our field of vision becomes altered in two ways: first, by my daughter, trudging home from school, pitched forward by the heft of her backpack; and second, by the reappearance of the drone, which has been out of sight and out of mind for some two weeks now. Tracking its approach, I experience that faint sense of conviviality one feels upon hailing a wayfaring vessel, along with the mild embarrassment that displaces it.

Saw, saw, saw, saw …

"Well holy hoppity hares," says Gresso, "look at that crazy shit fly!" And then, realizing Kira is within range, "Whoops, pardon my Portuguese, young lady."

"That's not Portuguese," she says, without lowering her eyes.

A second or two later, a text from Brooke arrives, "Any idea where S is, because he WAS NOT in his last 3 classes today," and I immediately peel off and begin stalking toward the hangar.

"Alrighty then, Jeff," yells Gresso, "I'll shoot an estimate over and you can tell me what you think." And while his words, his garrulous voice, aren't connected in any way to Simon's whereabouts and my rash, unidirectional supposition of the same, they have the effect of stopping me, rooting me in indecision … *Are you gonna crash in there, throw your weight around, play the hard-ass dad and landlord? Or will you leave it for later and spare him the open dressing-down—the precise misery of which, by the way, you have zero need to imagine?* I recall Brooke's semi-affectionate jab, "In fact, sometimes it's quite hilarious," and it is not at all lost on me that the gradation after hilarious is *pathetic*, and the one after that, *contemptible*, and so on, until you're not a father but an irrelevance, a hapless blusterer in a deafening wind.

And another consideration … I shouldn't need another, but one is swirling inside my head: namely, that purely from an actuarial standpoint, I am less likely to outlive the resentments held by my offspring than the average parent with the average quantity of platelets, white blood cells, and non-monoclonal proteins. Such is life outside the reference range …

"Daddy," Kira says with a yip and a gasp, and I lift my gaze just in time to see a small, coruscating object home in on and then obliterate the drone, momentarily filling the sky with fire and confetti.

There is no sound. Or perhaps the spectacle, with its considerable demands, has diverted the resources necessary to compile sound.

In the moment that follows, an assembly forms outside the hangar. A revivalist throng. I identify my son in its midst. Like the others, he rejoices. He emotes as if he were a child, which of course he still is, though in ways that are no longer malleable to me, if they ever were. Perhaps he authored the breakthrough, our aspiring Oppenheimer, the correction from failed beta to flawless launch.

Consequences notwithstanding—and they are bound to be grave—their proof-of-concept is now proven. In a month it will be crowdfunded. In a year it will be commercialized. In five it will be obsolete, as drones shed their heat signatures and acquire the capacity for tactical avoidance. And then the process begins again. Moving objects beget the forces that overtake them, given the time. That too can be actuarialized.

I become aware of Kira's hand in my own, her head against my shoulder. I'll hold on for as long as she'll allow and try not to worry about later.

FIELD NOTES FROM THE SPRING BIRD CENSUS

Though they live at the end of our lane, it's rare to catch sight of the Huffs other than in a passing car or by the rural mail post where the asphalt runs out. We welcomed them when they moved in, but they've kept themselves apart. Their property is twice the size and their house far grander than the others in our small plat of nine homes, so perhaps they are merely rising to their station. Their seclusion makes it difficult to know.

More so than the other neighbors, we have kept the lines open, and evidently with this day in mind, as here comes Taryn Huff, walking up our drive, gaze straight ahead, tensing herself for whatever mission has brought her this way. I call out to her so she won't be startled when she veers round the rockery to the paver path. Taryn, in my limited experience, is nearly always on edge, a filament of quick energy beneath her cutting eyes and taut, precise frame.

She snaps her head in my direction, locates a faint smile, waves. She is here to see Brooke, no doubt. Brooke has continued to make entreaties when the random opportunity presents, so there are those points of reference. She does this for the benefit of our daughter, as there exists a Huff girl of the same age. It is an enduring frustration for Kira that the only peer in shouting distance is all but inaccessible to her.

I let Taryn know that Brooke has gone out, and after a moment of indecision she skirts the low wall and steps along the path to where I'm kneeling. "I was hoping to settle up with Kira for watching Dexter last month," she says, and I am reminded that, yes, we were recently entrusted for several days with the care of their rabbit, meaning that after five years we've gained access to their hutch, if not their house.

I stand without dropping my tools, announcing in my own particular way that a more demonstrative greeting is impractical. This is basic hygiene with women who make me uneasy, and Taryn is certainly in that category.

"I'm pretty sure she's with Brooke," I say before realizing I can't be sure of that at all, Kira's whereabouts as a middle-teen falling increasingly outside the purview of a father's need to know. Or so she often reminds me. I get what I can from Brooke.

Taryn folds her arms, drums her fingers, bites her upper lip. She scans the yard, which isn't looking its best right now. She says, gesturing to the open transformer box and its jumble of loose wires, "So, what's going on here?"

Of course, she is not in the least interested, but, fine, something needs to be said, so I describe how I am trying to isolate a short in our landscape lighting. These are the dying days of men explaining things to women, though when it happens it can still arouse the senses. Close your eyes and you can almost catch a whiff of pipe smoke.

"Maybe I should come back later," she says and turns to leave.

"Wait," I say, far more sharply than intended, alarmed at losing the chance to engage her and imagining Brooke's unhappiness when she hears of it. I throw out the first thing that jumps to mind and ask after Garrett. She comes slowly back around, lets her gaze dwell on mine.

"He moved out a month ago," she says. "It's with the lawyers now."

I notice, after some lost number of seconds, that she's nodding, as though I have commiserated; expressed outrage; said something that has brought us into perfect agreement when I am unaware of having said anything at all. She goes on, "He hooked up with his personal trainer, of course, showing his complete lack of imagination," and the remainder of her story, insofar as she wishes to tell it, comes out in a few swift, scything strokes. Serial cheater; away all the time; "spousal neglect," to cite two highly specific, eye-opening words; joint funds offshored or gone missing altogether. That's what I catch.

I try to square this with my scant impressions of Garrett: athletic, darkly handsome, younger than Taryn; a financier of unspecified type; mastery of the quick, executive brush-off; an element of swashbuckle.

There is a clamor in the tree nearest to us and we both look up. It's the parrot. The large olive parrot that appeared here a few days ago and has roosted in our yard ever since. It yodels softly to us from a middle branch.

"What's that?" she says.

"A kea parrot, I think. I found some pictures online."

"What is it doing here?"

"No idea."

"But …"

"Yeah, I know," I say. "Doesn't make any sense. Must be someone's pet. I called Animal Control, but they weren't interested." Which, in fairness, is not an entirely accurate representation of their position. What the guy told me was, if I'm able to catch it, they'll take it in.

There is a moment where it feels like we might drift back to the topic of her marriage.

"Yesterday …" I begin to say and then pause to give thought. Five years of near unbroken silence and then an outpouring of woe. There is no context for what Taryn has just told me, except the universal context of reaching out, hoping for an ear. Has the parrot saved me from discomfort or diverted me from compassion?

"I'm sorry, what?"

"Yesterday, I was out here and went inside for a while … I think it stole my screwdriver."

"Oh," she says and begins nodding again. Not a normal nod. Like she's pounding nails with her chin.

"Anyway, sorry to hear about things on the home front," I say, trying hard not to look away. Casting around for something more, a supportive gesture, I smile and raise my hands to eye level, showing off my pliers and multimeter: "If you need any help over there, Taryn, just let me know. I promise not to break anything that isn't already broken." And a flood of pure, unfiltered magnanimity washes down from my prefrontal cortex and delivers a two-hundred proof hit of absolution.

"If I need any help?" she replies, her voice sending out a low, deathly whistle of accusation. "Help with what? Are you hitting on me? Oh my God, you're hitting on me, you are," and at this she begins to gag, back away, careen over the paving stones.

"Taryn," I begin to say, but she cuts me off, shouting, "What a jerk, what a lecher you are. All I wanted to do, all I came over here for … and you can't even restrain yourself for a second—"

"Restrain myself? What? What are you talking about?" I say, but she is already halfway down the driveway, hands over her ears, running for the street. I start after her and then stop, then yell out to her again, futilely. I tomahawk my pliers into the dirt, dropkick my multimeter across the lawn, rip off a blue streak that would cost me several levels of heaven if there were a just God to take notice of it.

Before I can settle down, the garage door opens, and Brooke rolls up in the wagon. "What's wrong?" she calls out, and I wave her off, in no great hurry to explain what just happened, especially with Kira in the seat next to her. She appears to say something in return, and then I realize it's the parrot, hectoring from the cottonwood across the road. I watch for a moment, trying to make sense of what I'm seeing. But it never really ascends to the level of doubt. Immediately beneath the ruffling bundle of drab green feathers, the leads of my multimeter dance limply in the breeze.

Brooke asks in a murmur when I plan to turn off my headlamp, and it is not an unreasonable question, given the hour. I drop the book I'm staring at, pull on my sweats, and slip downstairs. I go forty minutes on the stationary bike to skim off the froth still in my bloodstream. After several sets of crunches and a cool-down, I put in a couple of billable hours of work for a client, of which I have the tenuous quantity of one.

With my attention beginning to drift, I head outside to check on the stake lights. They're dead, of course. I pad over the lawn and climb to a perch atop the frontage berm, in the crosscurrents of the night air. Other than a sidelong moon, the only illumination in sight hovers over the church parking lot a half-mile to the east. A tent city was raised there several weeks ago, and the floods have remained on ever since. A security measure, apparently, though it's all fairly well organized, to my knowledge.

An intermittent bellow floats over from the Heaton parcel around the corner. They have several cows there, and it goes on like this when one or more of them is calving. Those cows have broken loose a few times, laying waste to our planted beds. You think of cattle as indiscriminate grazers, but they'll dine first and to utter completion on any available bounty of daylilies.

"What are you doing out there?" calls Brooke from the front door.

"Go back to bed," I tell her.

"Jeff, whatever went on with Taryn, it's fine now. She overreacted, she apologized … to me, anyway. You need to let it go."

"I'm working on it."

"Ah, then I'm sorry for interrupting," she says and lingers for a moment before fading back inside.

As I poke along the berm, something not entirely of mulch consistency rolls under my foot, and I find the remnants of a mole there, the second such discovery in the last two days. Gratification and disgust effervesce to a kind of tartness in my throat. The best type of mole is a decommissioned one, and even better if it doesn't have to be unskewered from an impaler trap. But I'd rather not have its guts in my runner treads.

Back inside, and with the resident fauna still on my mind, I post photos I've taken of the kea to a local bulletin board for missing pets. The only other found bird is a turkey. There is a video that shows it menacing patrons of a nearby mini mart, then repeatedly flogging its own reflection in the plate glass storefront. Even if someone owns it, I wouldn't think it qualifies as a pet. Toms can be incredibly hostile and are not really given to doting ministrations.

Still miles from sleep, I idly perform a search on Taryn's rogue husband. One match stands out, a Garrett Huff running a boutique hedge fund from offices in Seattle and San Francisco. Ex-Goldman, East Coast transplant, connections to various deal syndications, including a couple of notoriously odious ones dating to the last crash. Clearly it's him, though it is a little odd that he—that the family—landed in our sleepy little notch. Of course, the same could be said of us and certainly has been … not only by friends from our citified past but by Brooke and most especially me. The yearning for land may be intrinsic, but it isn't rational, and it can never be reciprocated. The grub shuns the mole, and the mole the rodentivore, but they and every other aspect of nature remain unified and implacable in defiance of our claim.

Heading upstairs, I consider waking Brooke to ask what she meant by the remark, "Whatever went on with Taryn." Nothing went on with Taryn. Nothing ever could go on with Taryn. Not that I am above imperiling my marriage in a blaze of rash stupidity. That could happen. That's a theoretical possibility, inside a helix of chromosomal code, atop a mountain of contextual history. But Taryn, for all her delft-like Netherlandic allure, her etherealness, vibrates with untethered nerves. It is hazardous enough to share the block with her—*as has just been proven out.*

With the sun nudging over the Cascades, I tumble into bed. Seconds later, a siren begins to whoop at the fire station—the station across from the church with the homeless encampment. As loud as it is for us, it must be an air raid inside the tents.

"You're back," Brooke says without opening her eyes. I wait for the racket to die down and then ask her, "How long are we planning to stay out here?" But it appears she has fallen asleep again.

Several days later I encounter one Garrett Huff, though it takes me a while to realize it. Spend enough time in coffee houses and you'll find yourself the object of the errant, searching gaze. It's part of the ecology there. It is easier to ignore if you have work to do, which I have, and a deadline, which is always *right away* for a freelancer. Yet now the guy eyeing me from across the room has approached to ask if we aren't neighbors, allowing me to make the connection and affirm that we are.

"The house on the slope, with the boy and the girl," he says with a note of admiration for his own insight.

"The girl looked after your rabbit recently," I remind him and then wonder if perhaps I shouldn't have. He may have already been booted out by then.

He sets down his coffee and pulls over a chair. Still smarting from my encounter with Taryn, I am on high alert. But he does the thing guys often do and inquires about my career, a subject on which there is embarrassingly little to say right now. When I put the question back to him, there is a lull, as though he is weighing my circumstances to determine if they merit the sharing of his own. Eventually he mentions the hedge fund, only hinting at the extent of his role there. The avoidance of ostentation, I can't help but feel, is a bookmark for its phantom presence.

"Does the fund have an emphasis?" I ask, opting for the least assuming among the list of reasonable next questions. Of course, Seattle, the Bay Area—what could it be except tech?

Again, the deliberative pause, the cryptic half-answer: "Not really an emphasis. More of a style; a distinguishing trait."

He looks away, surveys the space around us; pantomimes, in this way, his detachment, even though he's the one who came over in the first place. Garrett's world isn't altogether unknown to me, it so happens—something he should have gathered when he asked, and I answered, as to the name of my client. Even a hanger-on can know shit. And while making a show of this isn't my intent, I can't resist at least one small correction.

"Investors at that level generally aren't interested in style," I say.

"Yes and no," he tells me. "It's the things we do on the margins that attract money; that set us apart from our peer funds, who we otherwise resemble in most ways."

"What are you trading in that's so out of the main, Garrett? Misery bonds? Distressed currencies? I mean, you're already a hedge fund. People expect the risk, don't they?"

He tilts his head, smiles slightly—the notion occurring to him, for the first time, that I am not a financial illiterate. Leaning forward in his chair, he raises his *venti* cup an inch off the table, as if he's about to go queen to rook on my *macchiato*.

"One aspect of how we deploy capital," he says, "is in response to, or in anticipation of, or even through the shaping of government rule making. The recent changeover in the executive branch, especially, has broadened opportunities."

"I am sure it has," I say, more as a generalized acknowledgment of a dispiriting truth than as a conversational note.

He goes on, "Let me tell you about some of the more creative proposals we've seen recently, though not necessarily taken a stake in, just so you'll have the picture. Casino concessions in national parks; drone taxis to bring Mexicans over the wall; a gray market for school vouchers; a neural net model to refine voter-purge methodology; calamity enterprise structured on shoreline retreat or aquifer depletion or oil spills or fisheries collapse—"

"I'm detecting a certain theme here …"

"And then there's financial sector innovation, which has exploded in the current reg-rollback environment. Allow me to ask: have you ever heard of S.G.B.O.O's?"

"Heard of what?" I say while glancing at a text from Brooke. Something about our son.

"'Cig-booze,' phonetically, in industry parlance," he says. "It's beautiful, really, because the acronym captures both the fucked-in-the-ass symbolism of the cigar and the post-deal, self-congratulatory shot of Maker's Mark."

"You're losing me, Garrett."

"Securitized. Government. Bail-out. Obligations. If you're a hedge fund, or some other institutional or sovereign investor with access to dark markets, you can buy and sell these now. Essentially, securitized claims on future bailouts of too-big-to-fail banks. It was a huge missed opportunity in the last crash."

"That can't possibly be a real thing."

"Why not?"

"Because … because the government would have to pay twice. Once to settle up with the claim holders—you said it's an actual security, right?—and a second time to prop up the banks."

"Why only twice? There's no theoretical limit. Claims on TARP-style handouts for the same bank can be packaged and sold in tranches. The government might have to pay ten times the nominal bailout requirement. Or a hundred. And it will always pay. If it's Goldman, if it's Morgan or Citi or B of A, either as the risk holder or the counterparty, the government will always pay. Or the Fed will intervene and vacuum up the bile—same essential result."

I hold up my phone and say, "There is somewhere I have to be, Garrett," which, in fact, is true, though I also feel an overwhelming desire to get away from him and forget everything he just told me. I practically lost my livelihood in the last crash and have been scrambling ever since. The idea that there's a new class of derivatives capable of blowing up the world shouldn't surprise me, but there is an aspect of depravity to this one. A kind of Final Solution of wealth extraction for benefit of the already fabulously wealthy. He could be screwing with me, of course, but that would only mean they haven't gotten around to it yet.

Sitting inside the car, I again read the text from Brooke. Simon has mono and the university has suggested we bring him home for a week. Brooke is already on her way, so I'll have to fetch Kira from the pool and drive her to tutoring. My hands, I notice, are shaking slightly. And my TMJ might be acting up. Maybe Garrett just has this effect on people. Shutting my eyes and tilting back in the seat for a moment, I feel myself soften a little toward Taryn.

I spot a woman with a tripod near the stand of Doug firs along the south boundary of our property. She is peering through a mounted scope, which is aimed into the tree canopy. The county has had surveyors out here recently, which is never a good sign, so I jog down to see what I can find out. As I approach, she says, "You know what you've got up there?"

I look up, but before I notice anything, she continues, "That is a highly endangered bird, and quite a long way from home."

"Oh, is the parrot up there?" I say and am answered at once by a sharp, grating bleat from above, my obliviousness evidently taken as an affront. As if to affirm this, the parrot assumes a kind of phoenix pose, showing us the orange underside of its wing feathers.

"That's not just any parrot. It's an alpine parrot—a kea. They're found in only one place in the world, the South Island of New Zealand, and there aren't many of them left even there."

"How do you suppose …" I begin to ask, then notice an emblem on her field vest that seems to denote some sort of official status. I inquire about that first.

"I'm Dee, with the Cascadia Bird Club," she says, extending her hand. "Your posting has created an enormous stir among our members, so I have come out here to see if it wasn't a prank. This will play havoc with our annual census."

"Ah, you saw the photos, then."

"I didn't. Well, not initially. It just so happens one of our members lost her pug, and—"

"That's okay," I say, "I just wasn't sure how you found—us," for the first time including the parrot in the plural familiar. Odd, because he, or she, has spent less time on our property of late and more on our neighbors'. Maybe I'm feeling a bit possessive.

In the moment that follows, another interloper appears, this one emerging from the wetland trail across the road. At a glance I can tell he is not a bird spotter, and not only because of Dee's leery eye. More for the noticeable absence of fleece and the mismatched assemblage in its place. The parrot, too, has its qualms, erupting in a fit of complaint before tearing off down the lane and out of sight.

"That's Nestor, all right," the guy says as he ambles toward us. "There's only the one." And at this point I realize I've seen him before: in the lunch line at the tent city on the day we volunteered there with Kira's civics group. He's a kid, basically. A couple years older than Simon, or not even.

"Is that your parrot?" Dee asks with a tinge of reproof in her voice.

"Not my parrot, no ma'am," he says. "Such creatures are unclean and of a low order, despite their heavenly sojourn."

"Well, whose is it then?" she says with a small but emphatic foot stomp. "You certainly seemed to recognize one another."

"He belonged to Angel, for the most part. But Angel's dead a month already. I guess you could say he's his own bird now."

"Someone died up there?" I say, astounded.

"Uh, Angel … he accidently helped himself die, from what I gather. They were about to throw him out anyway. You can only have service pets in the camp. Nobody was buying that Nestor was a service pet. He did keep the vermin down, though."

"Vermin? What kind of vermin? Are you telling me it can hunt?" I say and immediately think of the now several vivisected moles I have come across over the last few weeks.

"Oh, sure," Dee chimes in, lapsing back into happy naturalist mode. "Keas are omnivores. In their native range, they're known to prey on live sheep."

We stand quietly for a moment. The sun sifts through the fir boughs, entangles us in light and shadow. From the direction of the wetland, an early-spring chorus of frogs rises and recedes.

My gaze wanders down again to Dee's insignia. Beneath the embroidered wren or nuthatch or feathered somesuch, and offset from the italicized society name, reads the epigram "Flock Together"—a whimsy that undermines her already suspect imprimatur. It is instinctual, isn't it, that we seek at times the stamp of authority, however obscure, so we can swallow the wholeness of truth. And even then … live sheep …

My mind ticks back to the conversation with Garrett Huff. I have been unable to confirm that S.G.B.O.O's exist, nor that they don't. So, from where would Garrett's authority derive? No doubt from my readiness to believe the worst—an easy thing to do given the banks, fund managers, and rating agencies that would have to be involved, and their reliably abhorrent tendencies. No officialdom necessary, though it could only help if they had an identifier of their own. I am imagining a fine Latinate scrawl in gold thread across an Italian suit lapel: *Member of the asshole class that only gives a fuck about itself.*

"There's nowhere I wouldn't go to actually see that happen," says our visitor from the itinerant side, snapping me back into the present.

"Well, then, let me tell you about the locale you'll have to travel to," Dee says and undertakes to do just that, riffing asides on habitat, climate zones, behavioral variation, and so forth.

The kid … this peculiar, gawky kid: whether or not he meant to be taken literally, he seems enthused that he has been. I remember that feeling, or something like it: broke, jobless, strange city, no one to give you the time of day until somebody does, and then *Wow, a listener!* This is going back decades now. I stayed above the dividing line somehow, the one this guy has already crossed. I mostly had luck to thank for that.

Catching Dee at an interlude, and trying to parlay the general air of conviviality, he says to me, "Nice chunk of property you've got here. Any chance you have some odd jobs for hire?"

"I'll need to get back to you on that," I tell him, coughing through my words. Translation: *Even if I do, I can't just spring this on Brooke.*

"I guess you know where to find me, then," he says.

Kira texts me while I am at the gym and asks if I'll feed the Huff rabbit, and rarely do I have an answer at the ready with such clarity as in this instance, "No." She types back, "Pls pls pls! Have swim practice after school Dex can't wait," to which I respond, "Still no."

Ten minutes later I receive a call from Brooke, who is in the Bay Area visiting her aunt. "Can you just go over there and do this for her? She was supposed to check on it yesterday and she didn't. The poor thing is probably starving by now."

"What if Taryn comes home while I'm there?"

"She's in Hawaii, Jeff, with Garrett, trying to save her marriage. That's why we're taking care of the rabbit again. Remember?"

I wander into the mat room, which is unoccupied, so I can hear over the whirring and clanging. There is a message spelled out in block letters on the opposite wall that reads "Who are you at your CORE?" I get the double-meaning, but it seems confrontational for a gym-wall koan. *Who the hell wants to know* is my first reaction, though admittedly I feel a touch put-upon right now.

"Jeff?" yoo-hoos Brooke, edging closer to provocation. The frisson from her minutely peaked brow zings through the phone and into my expertly tuned ear.

"I'm confused, Brooke," I say. "How do I go from 'lecherous jerk' to friendly neighborhood pet sitter in the span of a month?"

"Oh please, not again. Will you stop it with that?"

"If she seduces me while I'm there, it's on your conscience."

"Oh, yes. It would be on my conscience, wouldn't it? Unless you mean the rabbit, of course. It is a friendly little thing, but I am afraid it's a he, not a she."

Recognizing a last word when I hear one, I promptly give in and jump off the call so I can finish my workout. But I am distracted now and feel the need to put as much time as possible between the errand at hand and any potential Huff reappearance. After retrieving my gear, I head for the parking lot, scanning texts from Kira as I go: "… hutch in backyard … food in white bucket … hay in garden shed," and so forth.

I proceed directly to their house, slowing upon reaching the gravel drive that tunnels into their compound. Past the first curve, there are virtually no sightlines to the street or nearest neighbors, sheltered as the property is by a dense, 360-degree blind of giant firs and red cedars.

Leaving the car in the turnaround, and not having been here since the day we delivered a welcoming cookie plate five years ago, I take a minute to absorb the scene—noting first the darkened windows, the discreet signs noting 24-hour monitoring of the premises. Tracing the horizontal lines of the facade, I pan east to a terraced rise emerging into spring flower, then west to a meadow with a forked stone path that vanishes through a pair of detached gate arbors, their uprights enlaced in vines. Here and there lie islands of shrubs, feather grasses, and ornamental trees, many still in bud, and the occasional tortured bit of statuary. The overall tableau appears much as I remember it: a quiet, moody panorama resolving to a raked, modernist center point of concrete, steel, and exposed timbers. The Huffs have left well enough alone and seen to the upkeep.

Circling around back, I pass a fruit orchard rife with new growth and a curious, geometric arrangement of raised cultivation beds. The beds are new, but the orchard and surrounding deer-fence date to the previous owners. Not since they moved have we or the other neighbors been graced with the sacks of cherries, peaches, and apples that would appear on our doorsteps unbidden, a deprivation we all still rue. Pie production on this block has never recovered.

Feeling at this point no great rush to be done here, I continue along the pebble track that leads to a creek running along a remote segment of the property line. As wet as winter and spring have been, the current should be swift, and indeed it is. In certain lucky years there'll be kokanee paddling upstream, and in the pre-Huff days I would come down here with the kids to watch for them. We knew we were always welcome.

When they left—the prior owners—we considered, very briefly, trying to buy this place. That was more fantasy than reality at the time. It occurs to me now that we might soon get another crack at it. Would Taryn really stay here on her own?

Walking back toward the residence, I miss the hutch at first and then find it: a two-story wood and wire structure situated inside a converted dog run. The gate to the dog run is slightly ajar, and a bubble of concern immediately inflates in my chest. Stepping inside, I snatch up a ladle lying next to the sealed food bucket and begin poking around in the clumps of straw and timothy hay scattered throughout the hutch. Nothing. I unclasp the top hatch and drop the ladle into a walled-off compartment of the upper level, swinging it from side to side. Again, nothing. The food bowl contains a single, unmolested pellet; the water reservoir is nearly dry.

I text Kira—"Hutch inside dog run, right? And rabbit inside hutch?"

"Hops around pen when sees me coming. So cute!"

"Pen?"

"Pen where hutch is!"

I try phoning Brooke, who doesn't answer, which is just as well given my instantly searing displeasure. I start thrashing through the surrounding vegetation, thinking it might be close and is attuned to certain basic, determinative aspects of inserting itself into the food-chain. And will a rabbit respond to its name? I begin calling it regardless, interspersed with modifiers that might also sound familiar if it reads Elmore Leonard novels, perchance, or plays hockey in a beer league.

The rabbit is alive, and the rabbit will be found—on these points I refuse to negotiate. There is not a speck of blood in that enclosure, not a tuft of fur, neither canine print nor cat whisker. And don't tell me the parrot slid that bolt latch, because that's not happening, even if it does have my screwdriver. Kira left the gate open and it shimmied out. Or maybe a landscaper swept off the concrete and neglected to lock up.

With the morning light shifting in my favor, I expand my search in an ever-widening radius, eventually rustling through every sprig of undergrowth within fifty yards of the house. A pair of fraught ground nesters, one spindly tree frog, several burrowing bees, a working termite farm at the base of a rotting stump … such are the contents of my dragnet when I stop to reassess. Kneeling in the grass by the arbor path, I weigh first the contextual question, *Is this a rational response to my predicament*, and then its more prodding corollary, *Is it apt to achieve its intended result?* Brooke has encouraged me to do this over the years, to try not to fixate or spin around in my own dust cloud; to climb up for a better view. I have made strides with the self-awareness part but often lack the equanimity to let go … the rabbit *is* nearby, *I can sense it*. The uneaten morsel is a postcard, a troll for our inattentive care. But maybe—and, all right, perhaps this is evidence of personal growth in real time—maybe it's not only a troll but a signal for how, in this case, redemption might be attained, calamity unwound. Fill the bowl, at least; replenish the water dropper; lay in some fresh bedding. See what happens.

By the time Brooke checks in to ask why I called, I have cleaned and prepared the hutch for a royal return to estate. Just doing this, completing these simple, earthly tasks, is restorative; injects me with optimism and neighborly spirit; allows me to take solace in having done what I can. After laying out the situation for Brooke, in a manner as composed and affirmative as I genuinely feel, she says, this woman I have been married to for more than twenty years, and whose range of sentiment I often fail to account for … she says to me, each word a frozen shard of mortal threat: "I don't care what you've already done. I don't care what you do next. But they fly home on Sunday. And the rabbit will be in its cage when they arrive. It will be there."

Seeing the rain let up, I set off for the church on foot, taking the wetland trail that connects to the expanding civic campus just east of our neighborhood. The stillness of the morning belies the trill and chatter emanating from the grassy, meandering bog. Steam rises from its various hot spots, tapers into the subdued light.

Reaching the base of the hill, I discover the ascent paved and come upon two new picnic shelters situated at one of the natural landings. It's further evidence of the encroachment here, what with the cluster of public amenities—library, community center, county services office—and the relentless sprouting of nearby subdivisions.

The tent city is an aspect of this too, I suppose. The church stands next door to the library.

As I duck through a hedgerow that separates the adjoining properties, I find the encampment gone, the parking lot scoured. A van sits in the fire lane, its rear door open. A woman emerges from the church carrying a flat of water bottles and steps over to the van. Freeing her hands, she waves in my direction and smiles. It could be we have met at some point or seen each other around town. Despite all the new arrivals, that sense of benign recognition still pervades here: in shops, in schools, almost anywhere people gather.

"Nice to have a break from the deluge," she says as I stroll toward her. I let her know I agree but hold back on the high spirits. We've had rain for most of the last week, and every glance upward has seemed to invite a fresh downpour.

"I see all the tents are gone," I say without specifically stating my business for being there.

"Yes, the permit for the camp was temporary, and the city declined to renew it. They're in Kirkland now, at one of our sister facilities. Had you come here to volunteer?"

"I am afraid not," I say, always quick to sidestep any attribution of altruism lest it lead to something deeper than I might like it to. This is particularly true when visiting those places most apt to promote such entanglements.

At a bit of a loss over what to do, I wish her a nice day and begin to retrace my steps. I had a plan, and now that plan is dead, which was to see if the homeless kid, whose name, I have come to learn, is Ethan, might want to change out some fence boards for me. I have the lumber, the galvanized nails, a sharpened saw blade, and the cash to pay him, which I didn't have last time … last time being when I practically dragged him out of his tent to help search for the rabbit—this, after Brooke's clarifying words to me. He staggered away after a half hour, having wandered into a nettle patch and complaining the task was beneath him, which I couldn't really deny. He'd asked if there were any "odd jobs for hire," not to go on a snipe hunt.

"Please give my regards to Brooke," the church lady calls out, and I improvise an acknowledgment to suggest I know who she is and have known all along. Just another day as the hermit husband of an everywhere wife.

With my good intentions burning a hole in my hat, I plop down on a bench under one of the picnic shelters to brood. The back and forth to Kirkland for a couple of hours of make-work seems excessive. I still owe Ethan a few dollars for his time, but he left without asking for it, so I doubt he cares. Maybe the larger debt he's due is for his parting innovation, which was to suggest I deploy a couple of box traps. Simple carrot-and-string box traps. "Anyone knows that's how you snag a rabbit," he said with open indignation. "You can't just go chasing after 'em."

The traps did work, if not exactly in the manner intended. When Kira and I went to check on them a final time, only hours before the Huffs were due back, one of them had indeed dropped. As I tipped up an edge to peek, the parrot lunged out at me, and I don't doubt that it would have dragged me under and made salad if it wasn't tangled in the string. Once my heart began beating again, I dashed home for a scrap of plywood, and we carried off the trap like Pharaoh's litter. The next day the parrot was in the custody of a local sanctuary, safe if not altogether sound … but better off, anyway, than a certain confounding rabbit. It is possible old Dex is still on the loose, though his lack of street smarts does not bode well, not in this area. Raptors, snakes, coyotes, bobcats—we've got them all, and woe to any varmint that drops its guard for a second.

Thinking I should head home and do some work today—the kind that pays—I shove off down the trail, scrolling through messages as I go. There is a thread from Garrett Huff I've ignored for days, and I have to read it twice, as he rambles on a bit before coming to any discernible point. He sounds a little lost, frankly. He mentions that the reconciliation with Taryn didn't work out, something Brooke has already told me, then pokes around for any inside information about current goings-on at his house—information that I willfully, enthusiastically, do not possess.

Near the end, he writes, "I heard about the business with the parrot. We should talk about New Zealand. I'm scouting for an evacuation bunker there, along with everyone else in my line of work who's looking ahead. Better that than on the tines of a pitchfork, right? So maybe we'll be neighbors again."

Well, yes, maybe we will, thanks to Kira, who recorded the harrowing, gloved transfer from box trap to bird carrier, courtesy of the sanctuary guy, and then immediately hit "Share," sparking a meme that has become a brushfire. Now there's a conservation group in Queenstown lobbying to confer citizenship—and a Royal Order of Merit!—on the Yank who snared a kea in an apple crate. Which I am not discouraging. More than ever, it seems important to have a backup plan, and you could do worse than a temperate, arcadian sweep of high ground with a thousand-mile moat in all directions and plenty of cheap, respectable wine. Of course, the prospect of being surrounded by New York bankers over there, that's not really a selling point, is it?

Crossing the street to our house, I find my son shooting hoops in the driveway. Finals done last week, home till September, plans TBD. He barely acknowledges me, per usual, but we quickly fall into a game of horse. He starts in with all the moves he's sure I can't do anymore—reverses, double pumps, rim touches. When he clangs the potential winner, I take him deep and run him up to S. He scoffs … lets me know, in this way, that this is all a bother to him. That's all right.

I'm ready to have him home for a while. When he leaves for good, and then his sister, we'll find out if we're truly rooted here, Brooke and I will. City life still beckons, though that might be our younger selves sharing a laugh at our expense.

AFTERGLOW

While approaching an empty intersection on the north side of the plateau, I see a bloom of violet light fluxing over a high-voltage line where it terminates inside the local substation. It can't be a normal event, so I slip into a parking lot across the street for a longer look. A shrill, magnetic hum is audible from this distance, yet seems oddly dissociated from the color effect, which is amoebic and ghostly.

I step out of the car and tap a few photos, but the image doesn't translate well. Neither does a short video when I try that too. Damp as the night is, a kind of synaptic chaos is visible as mist sways inside the aura.

Navigating to the power company's "Report an Issue" page, I find an automated way to indicate a residential outage but no obvious means to note spectral phenomena hovering over some random switchgear. Before I can resolve this, a kid retrieving shopping carts comes up near to me and stops to take in the sight across the road. He says, after a moment of quiet observation, "We just learned about this."

"Learned about what?" I ask when it becomes apparent that elaboration isn't necessarily forthcoming.

"Ionized air glow. Essentially, escaped current reacting with air and moisture. It's characterized by emissions of photons on the infrared scale. That's why it's purple, I think."

"Is it combustible?"

"I'm not sure. I'll have to ask my professor. I mean, assuming we don't get an answer right here and now."

As he completes this thought, the illumination winks out, and the sound dies down to a less alarming apiarian buzz—a consolation in the larger scheme of things, if somewhat of an anticlimax, which the incidental physicist to my left appears to feel more keenly.

"Too bad," he says, and then, unrelatedly, and with a little more engagement in his immediate surroundings, "You're Simon's dad, aren't you?"

"Sorry, have we met?"

"I remember seeing you at Eastlake cross-country meets a few years ago. Cheering him on."

"Oh, right. I went to a lot of those."

"Tell him Conor says hey."

"Okay."

"Conor H., that is. There were like five Conors on that team."

"I'll tell him."

Hours later, three successive explosions split the night air and lift me out of the disordered beginnings of sleep. While it is not unheard of for a certain neighbor of ours to fell a deer from his patio, the backup light on our security display confirms the loss of power. Those booms were almost certainly line transformers blowing one after the other, which instantly calls to mind the psychedelia on view at the substation.

Brooke rolls over and sighs, yet somehow doesn't fully wake up. Amazing, considering the shock wave effect on the house and windows. Seconds later my phone vibrates, and it's a text from Rolf, the husband of one of Brooke's fast friends. They live several blocks away.

"That loud enough for you? No power here."

Without replying, I slip out to the guest bedroom to scan the street. There is one transformer we have a sight line to, and I get a fix on it just in time to see it plummet to the ground, consumed in flames. I fly downstairs and out of the house, hopping into my sweats and runners along the way, barely avoiding a face-plant while attempting to clear the front stoop. By the time I make it to the end of the block, Sid and Varun, whose properties are closer, are already there, their faces illuminated by the candlepower flowing off the smoldering metal housing.

"Usually it's just the frogs at this hour," Varun says, alluding to the racket that emanates this time of year from the wetland east of our plat.

"They've gone quiet," Sid points out. "Is that all we need to do? Set off fireworks every evening before we turn in?"

"Maybe they think it's a bigger frog," I say.

"Hah! Yes, and that the courtship battle is lost for the night. Might as well give it a rest."

The impact from the fallen tank has fractured the bare earth underneath, and while there is now a shallow, meteoric crater there, nothing else is close enough, or perhaps dry enough, to catch and burn—my main concern when I saw the thing drop. Thirty feet above, surge arresters and frayed wires dangle in the dark.

Varun mentions he has some safety cones in his shed, courtesy of the prior homeowner, so the two of us head over there and fish them out. We situate them around the tank and run painter's tape from one to the other. I draw his attention to the Puget Sound Energy lettering on one of the cones and he laughs. "They are welcome to reclaim them."

Having done what we can, I quit for home, and Sid and Varun shove off in the other direction … the two of them with their glossy bald heads that generate a certain wattage of their own. Fifty yards along, the bite of scalded insulating oil remains far up my nose, though I may be carrying it with me.

I linger a moment outside the house. The din from the wetland has indeed settled down. The coyotes are mum, too. As is the saw-whet owl I first heard a week ago whose song so closely resembles the warning signal from a truck in reverse that I assumed that's what it was. But hardly a peep right now. It's as if the night and its swarms have been vanquished. Only faint rustles here and there in the cool dark.

Brooke mutters while I am slipping beneath the covers, "Are you just now coming to bed?"

I pause a minute and then say, "There should be some way to collectivize deep sleep, to account for inequities. It would solve a lot of problems."

"Oh?"

"Our recently dethroned petty tyrant slept four hours a night while he was in the White House. Maybe he needed more REM."

"Mmm … his problems ran a little deeper, I think. You need more, though."

"You're right about that."

"Anyway, come closer. I'll try to share."

I drop my phone and scoot over, shaking my head over the last thing I saw on my screen: a long screed from Rolf about Cozy Bear hacking our grid. Our little burg up here in the foothills, I guess we're a soft target.

"Am I making dinner tonight or are you?" asks Brooke in a meter I well understand. While she heads upstairs to shower, having hoed weeds the last couple of hours, I commence rooting around the kitchen. It is during this time that Simon, whose work schedule and careful parent-avoidance strategies make him a rare sight these days, ghosts into the room.

"Conor from your XC team says hello," I tell him.

"Which one?"

"Conor H."

"There were two of those, but okay. I think I know."

"He must have some high-concept major, that kid."

"Probably so. I go against him in *Gwent* sometimes. He's pretty savvy."

"*Gwent*, right," I say, absentmindedly, and immediately realize my tone was wrong.

He studies me for a moment, dolefully, then turns away. Guessing, correctly, that I have forgotten everything he explained to me about *Gwent* the one time I prevailed on him to try. It seemed impossibly complex, and, to be honest, any hope for enlightenment died in the telling of it. It remains a thing my son does, along with his gig at REI and mining digital currency, instead of completing his degree, having dropped out of UBC more than two years ago. That's all it can ever be.

"Maybe you should call Conor," I say before he is out of earshot. "You know, like, go for a run or something"—making the situation worse, I am sure, but I have learned that it is better to confine scourge father and solicitous father to their discrete forms rather than admix them, in which case every interaction would be bad.

Further on in the evening, I invoke Conor H. again, this time while seated around a firepit at Varun and Amrita's place. Other neighbors have dropped by, too, and we've come around to the blown-transformer business from earlier in the week. I describe, as best I can, the sight at the substation, as well as the impromptu scholarship it gave rise to, and I earn scoffs left and right.

"Doesn't know what he's talking about" and "Nothing at all to do with the outage" and "Surely something more commonplace, a corona discharge, perhaps" and so forth. It is here that I should make mention of the higher-than-average number of polymaths who have settled on the plateau, even in our semi-rural tract, many on visas from faraway shores where they attained such learning, nearly all of whom work at Microsoft or Amazon or one aerospace firm or another. Thus the flaunting of STEM chops, in which I, an elder among this group and the son of an electrician, who knows black wires go with black but not very much else, cannot hold my own and know better than to try. Beyond that, I feel strangely, if silently, allegiant to the "Purple Rain" thesis, evoking as it does a kind of simple, ethereal beauty equal to the vision itself.

"Some guy has ranted for days on Nextdoor that it's a Russian ransomware attack," says Sid, to which I add precisely nothing lest he or the others guess that it is a friend of ours … if only nominally, by sisterly association. Not that it is impossible, I suppose, the prospect of a malicious hack. But Rolf has a history of half-cocked conspiracy theorizing, and it makes it difficult to take anything he says seriously. If I pose the sleep-transference idea to him, he'll tell me it's already happening and that Bill Gates is the one behind it.

From the outer circle, I overhear Amrita ask Brooke how Simon and Kira are doing, and she tackles the Kira part first because, of course, that's easier, everything is terrific, good grades, fun boyfriend, loves it down in Portland, activities and study groups for every pinhole in her schedule, probably too many, but that's Kira, and she always makes it work. Simon gets the "He has plenty of time to figure it out" treatment, and he does, certainly, and I want to jump up and add, *steady job, doesn't do drugs, reads discerningly, is gentle with kids, pets, and insects for that matter, has a sympathetic soul and telescoping mind,* but, truth be told, I'd shoot off confetti guns right now if he were to enroll in a class, join a meetup, find a pickup game, or ask a co-worker to a movie. Any small gesture that might carry him outside his self-enclosed world.

Gwent and other such diversions consume scalar hours each week. The cryptocurrency mining goes on day and night, whether he is at home or not, as he built a separate server to handle the churning and saves his other rig for gaming.

"If you continue on with that," I told him, once I caught on to his foray into the realm of distributed blockchain, "you'll have to reimburse us for the energy costs and buy carbon offsets too," which, calling my bluff, he has actually done, though the offsets are of dubious origin, and I've grown skeptical of the entire premise. *If you'll save that tree, I can burn this pile of coal,* yeah, that solves everything.

Maybe, in some circuitous way, his amperage spikes, along with those of others nearby—he's not a one-off, there are plenty of young shutaways reigning over galaxies from their pixel-illuminated bedrooms—blew up the city's power block. It's something to consider, anyway.

"You look like you're ready to go home," Brooke whispers, attentive as always to minute changes in atmosphere. At least when she's awake. We bid our goodnights and tread along the fence line to our wooded acre and a half. City creatures in our world-beater days, we have come to appreciate our landing spot up here. Doug firs rule the high ether, hemlocks and cedars lurk one story down. The Cascades, of which we reside at the humble toe, paint our easterly views. Olympics to the west.

"That was Rolf they were joking about, wasn't it?" Brooke asks.

"None of them know him personally, but yes."

"It's sad, even Zhi is a little out there now. She's definitely cooler to me since the election. I always thought she quietly accepted that her husband was a crank, not that she agreed with him on anything."

"Well, in her case, I guess we really can say Stockholm syndrome. He's a Swede, isn't he?"

"*Deutsch.*"

"Oh, hmm. If you go back to the Bronze Age, though …"

As we approach the house, we see a faint, familiar screen-glow glancing off Simon's bedroom window. How fantastical are his dreams, I wonder, or do they fail to measure up.

I know who is texting me before I pick up my phone because this is when we often chat, when her mother is lights-out and I am the only one available.

"You're up late," I say.

"How old was I when Rena died?" she asks, referring to Brooke's mother.

"You were nine, why?"

"Couldn't remember, that's all."

I could try to excavate here, because something brought this on, but I am pretty well versed in how this goes. It's past midnight, she is alone in her dorm room, her mind is drifting; still winding down from a whirlwind day, the only kind she knows. It is a very Kira-type question at a Kira-type moment.

"Saw Varun and Amrita's kids tonight," I tell her, the proper names of her former babysitting charges eluding my drowsy mind. "They asked for you."

She responds with hearts as I knew she would. She is fond of them.

"How are Mom and Simon?" she types a moment later.

"You've asked that question to tease me," I say after I set down my book, turn off the reading lamp, and lay back my head. "You talk with them more than I do, especially your brother," to which she replies with a smirky face. These conversations never really end, they just wander along until she can sleep. When she can, I can, sometimes.

Maybe a quarter hour after I last hear from her, a familiar sound blows through the curtains, a bit later than usual. Neither lovelorn frog nor rapturous canine nor shy, nocturnal whistler. A middle-scale note, floating down from the north, played on a trumpet with a Harmon mute, and drawn out until it collapses into an exhausted sigh. Not literally, of course, but that's the impression it leaves. There must be a dozen recordings of Miles holding that same note, so the association is easy to make.

Fifteen years we have lived here, and it has pricked at me for the longest while: what is it, actually?

Well, I do have a thought, arrived at some time ago, wholly unburdened by scientific merit. The market across from the substation … as with all such food emporiums, semis dock there at night to off-load for the following day. And one particular cabbage hauler, opting for the southbound approach up Lowhills Drive, would have to contend with the short, precipitous drop from its summit to a traffic stop diagonal to the store parking lot. That's the sound of compression brakes, modulated by distance, windspeed, moisture in the air, and, oh, I don't know, rogue photons crisscrossing in the dark, dashing the sky violet …

Or, what … something else.

I could seek opinions from my neighbors, but I haven't, and no sense asking them now. I'll wait until I run into Conor H. again, he works at that market. We'll see what he has to say.

NO LIVING MEMORY

We depart the hotel in Crescent City just before 9:00 a.m. and drive south along the coast. Sections of the road are washed out, and we have to wait at times to proceed single file through the traffic barriers. Preserved stands of redwood, quiet inlets and sloughs, and sweeps of rocky shoreline are often in view, so we're fine with the meandering pace. With trailheads at almost every turnoff, it is easy to imagine a day different than the one laid out for us.

After a stop in Eureka to claim Lonny's ashes, along with the seventeen thousand in cash the coroner found in his apartment, we continue on to Garberville, an hour further down 101 and thirty miles or so inland, where we have coffee and buy something to eat for later. Brooke is pensive but hardly seems overcome, not in any way you could tell.

She says to me while we are still loitering on the back patio of the espresso shop, "The sergeant on duty, when he handed me the money, he said, 'Welcome to Humboldt County.'"

"That's a line from *Murder Mountain*."

"It seems strange, his just letting me walk out with it. When I offered to show him my ID, he told me, 'I know

who you are. And I know you're his only living relation.'
They've done their homework, evidently."

"If he has a hundred dollars in a bank account, we'll need a sworn affidavit to get it. So maybe currency is treated more like personal effects? And if there's not a will ..."

"He said for sure there isn't."

The remainder of the drive takes us west over the hills, through the progressively smaller and more amorphous communities of Redway, Briceland, and Whitethorn. I have made this trip once before, and there is a sense of disappearance, of an enveloping remoteness as you coil higher and deeper into the forest. There are still redwoods here, though they're crowded by other species in a way that is less common farther north—perhaps because they are not so definitively the apex flora in this area as they are along the mist belt of Del Norte and the southwestern corner of Oregon.

Outside the town centers we pass through, such as they are, there are few signs of life other than unmarked dirt driveways that are immediately swallowed by shadows and overgrowth. I can't help but wonder at the dense and verdant nature of the terrain, untouched by fire. That almost certainly won't last, given how much of California is burning every year.

At the westernmost boundary of Whitethorn, we locate its modest, single-manned post office. The coroner, during his sweep of the apartment, had gathered up the assorted keys he came across, and among them was one for a PO box. While Brooke is inside returning the key and processing the forwarding address, a tattered old guy with a cane hobbles along, looks me up and down, and says, "You're here from S.F."

"Wrong direction," I tell him, neglecting to mention that we very well used to be, while at the same time wondering what it is about my jeans and canvas jacket that has allowed him to genotype me. Or perhaps it's the car, with its clean sheet metal and tread on the tires. "We're in from the Seattle area," I add.

"Need directions to someplace?" he asks, likely more out of curiosity than altruism. Or so I have the sense.

"You must know the area pretty well," I say, rather than answer him directly.

"Been here forty years. I ought to."

I do the quick calculation. That's about when Lonny moved up here, to the best of our understanding. Brooke hasn't seen or heard from him for at least that long. This guy could easily have known him, or certainly known of him, even accounting for the anonymity so many come here for in the first place. Four decades past, there weren't that many souls to keep track of in these woods. I imagine that's changing, with legalization, but even now it feels like hermitville to me.

Zoning back in, I realize my helpful passerby is still waiting for an answer. With so much cash in the car, and being mindful of our present environs, there is a limit to the information I am willing to share. Fortunately Brooke reappears, and I signal to him we'll be moving on. I briefly consider offering him a few dollars, but he doesn't ask for any, and it dawns on me that I am engaging in a little stereotyping of my own.

"Don't stop for sightseeing," he calls out as we pull away. "Or anything else. Not till you're off the mountain."

———

The drop down into Shelter Cove levels off to a curving beach access road that runs past a marina and a small lighthouse. We pull into an empty parking area between the two and carry our lunches to a picnic table situated on a grassy bluff. A set of wooden stairs descends the fifty feet or so to the actual beach, and while we don't presently head down, the mental note is made for later. Brooke has no intention, I am utterly sure, of chauffeuring Lonny's ashes to Seattle, much less safekeeping them when we get there.

In the time it takes us to unwrap our sandwiches, several seabirds glide in for a landing and begin side-eyeing us from a respectful distance.

"I think that's his apartment, the one right over there," Brooke says, pointing to a split shingled, three-story edifice less than a quarter mile away. "I recognize it from Google Earth."

Straight as a cake box, joined on both sides by vast, empty lots, and with the first story being essentially a covered parking bay on stilts, the entire structure appears to judder in the wind, which is blowing in apace from the southwest. The landlord, Kato, who I have been in touch with, told me Lonny had the upper floor. And while the building itself is unassuming in every respect, the view from on top would have to be glorious—a wide-open panorama of the whole North Pacific, if your eyes could gather in that much.

Taken by the same thought, Brooke says, "He didn't suffer for natural wonder in his waning years. It's beautiful here."

"A couple of months from now the whale pods will be cruising by. It's like Point Reyes or Point Pinos: you'll be able to sit on a rock and keep count."

"I wonder if he was the type to have done that. To appreciate splendor. Somehow I can't project anything on to him in the way of raised consciousness."

"You can be excused for that."

"I don't mean it in a judgmental way. Just that I have tried to imagine it and nothing comes. It's a blank for me."

Having hardly touched her food, she steps over to the edge of the bluff. It is not a particularly violent sea, but scattered outcrops push up the water in bursts of spray and foam. A pair of trawlers tack slowly to the north several hundred yards offshore.

Lonny cut out on Brooke and her mother when she was two. Showed up once, several years later, for an hour-long visit she wasn't the focus of and scarcely remembers—presumably right before he decamped for Whitethorn and a livelihood in cultivation. He never wrote, never called. Withdrew from nearly all earthly contact, inasmuch as she was aware … though, in a practical sense, that was also the case for her beforehand. *A blank for me*, as she just said.

Not entirely for me, though. On a road trip through the north counties with my brother, we got it into our heads to go looking for him, and find him we did. Living in a broken-down barn on homesteaded land. Heating and cooking with propane. Keeping stores in an ice chest. A couple of murderous hounds who would have gladly made chaff out of us had he let them. We never saw his grow, but we knew it was there. Enough to pay for his needs, ascetic as they plainly were. This was twenty years ago now.

Brooke was in L.A. that weekend to see college friends; would have said to leave him be, had we asked. She would have been right, of course. The phone number I gave him, the address, they went unused. We moved, the thread was lost. Simon, our boy, was a small fry at the time. He turned twenty-three this year. The picture I had in my wallet, I left it there.

"We should probably get started," Brooke says as she approaches the table, and I am happy to agree. We've given ourselves a single day to tend to our business here, and more than half of it is already gone. Making it back over the mountain by sunset is the priority and was so even before our impromptu lecture outside the post office.

The birds close in on us as we gather up our things, but they'll soon be disappointed.

We're intercepted on the middle landing by Lonny's neighbor, who tells us Kato rekeyed the lock and has asked him to let us in. He is a buff guy in his thirties or forties with a wispy goatee and a helpful manner. He seems eager to confide what he knows and says straight off that he's the one who called the sheriff after noticing how quiet it had become upstairs.

"I walked in right behind them and saw him kind of half lying down on the sofa. His arms were crossed over his chest, and he looked peaceful to my eye. They told me later he'd passed a couple days before."

We learn, before we even make it to the top floor, that Lonny moved here seven or eight years ago, having divested his stake up in Whitethorn; that he was "spry as hell" for a guy of eighty-three; that the maroon Ford Ranchero in the driveway, rusting to bits in the sea air, was his ticket to neighboring towns when he had business to take care of or an appointment at the clinic in Redway.

"I'd offer him a jump if he needed one, which was whenever he tried to start that thing. That's mostly when we'd talk. When we were working on the trucks, I mean. Mine or his."

Brooke asks if Lonny had visitors, and he says, "Only one, generally speaking. That's Mim. She'll be coming by. I saw you pull up out front, and I let her know you were here."

He waits attentively for a follow-up question, but Brooke leaves it where it is. She thanks him for keeping an eye out for Lonny and befriending him as he did. As we are about to enter the apartment, he turns at the railing and says, "Yeah, another thing I should tell you: Lonny, he had money buried somewhere, back up the mountain. Probably a lot. Knowing the man as I have … no one'll ever find it."

This revelation, the timbre of it … it's like being wakened by the sound of the surf while dreaming of the beach you're lying on. As soon as you hear it, you realize you expected to hear it. For every dollar buried in this county, there is the legend of a thousand more and a hidden map to nowhere. Maybe this time it's real, maybe not. Lonny has already covered the cost of our trip, and his own final journey as well, and I am not about to begrudge him more. As for Brooke, her injury cannot be compounded. Not after so long and so little.

The inside of the apartment, at first glance, could be worse, though not by very much. Someone had the foresight to leave the two seaward windows cracked, saving us from the aspect we dreaded most: the reek of rooms closed up for two weeks after carting out a moldering body. Beyond that, it is disheartening, and I find myself trying to blur the details. Suffice to say that a long, long time has elapsed without a thought to cleaning or straightening or discarding what should obviously be discarded.

"Remember what we came here for," I say as I notice Brooke trying to compose herself: namely, to gather up records and correspondence and such so we are able to settle his affairs. There is the prospect for some closure, too, though I remain skeptical of the concept on the whole, haunted as I am by paternal affronts of my own. Still, anything that might bring her peace is welcome, and I am ready to encourage the process if I can.

The next two hours unfold in a more or less methodical way as we fill file boxes with documents, none of which are organized in any discernible manner, just lying loose atop or beneath or inside the various solid surfaces we find in the two main rooms—a desk, a table, a dresser, a steamer trunk, a bookcase with no actual books, all of it and everything else looking as if it was collected from the roadside next to a "For Free" sign.

We find very little of personal interest to dwell over. No pictures, no journal, nothing hung on the walls. No watch, almost no trinkets at all—a complete absence of effects that would imply any element of vanity. No tax returns, which can convey a certain biography of their own. There is an antique terrestrial globe on a bronze spindle and a worn, heavily marked set of world topographical maps, hinting at an avocation of sorts. Also, stashed in a cigar box, his dog tags, there amid detritus not really worthy of the shared space.

"He was field medic," Brooke says, separating the tags in her palm, then tracing a finger along the bead chain. "My mother must have told me that."

Lonny's service time would have come after Korea and before Vietnam. In this way he lucked out; in others emphatically not, to hear Brooke describe it. To wit: an alcoholic mother; a crackpot, government-hating father. She never knew them either, so the context for her is all at a remove.

"What's interesting to me is how little she told you overall," I say.

"I think, because he wasn't present in my life, and he wasn't present by choice, which I must have had a sense of—I am not sure how much I asked. Even as a child, I felt an aversion to doing that."

"Not every kid would have responded that way. The standard psych-book trope—isn't it of the son or daughter who idealizes the missing parent?"

"Yes, I am aware of that. But maybe, and I don't know … I was so close with my mother and my grandparents—her parents. That gave me a lot to fall back on. And my mother … her attitude toward Lonny was so detached, so devoid of sentimentality or anger or any vestiges of heartbreak, at least outwardly. That was my model."

Reorienting her gaze, she drops to one knee and slides a foil sheet pan from beneath the lowest desk drawer where I had shoved it with my foot, and I already know a second one lies behind it. They hold contraband of a quantity and vintage to suggest Lonny had not yet fully retired.

"And then there's this," she says, running a hand through her hair and speaking from a place of almost endless resignation. "It is the defining thing I have known about him for most of my remembered life. That he was a grower up in the emerald triangle."

We had already guessed Lonny still had plants some-where. The cash the coroner recovered was the first clue, and we've found another twelve hundred he missed, rolled up in jacket pockets, clothes drawers, tea tins, and so forth. On its own that's not dispositive, but the fragrance we waded into as soon as we stepped through the door has proven to be—and with no sign of his having joined the new economy, where such activity might be presumed legal.

We begin, after a bit more searching and sorting, to carry the boxes down to the car, along with other items Brooke deems worthy of rescue, only the globe not fitting into the trunk. On one of these trips, I find Brooke standing at the curb with a woman in her seventies, or thereabouts. Stained red parka, plaid shirt, drawstring pants. Someone who was likely only ever petite but is now starkly shrunken in appearance. This is Mim, I learn, Lonny's friend of a type.

Brooke hands me a pocket folder and tells me I can drop it into one of the boxes. Before doing so I look inside: photographs—perhaps ten or twelve altogether. Some, we are told, belonged to Mim, others she collected from the apartment before Kato changed the lock. Lonny appears in most of them. A younger Mim does as well, along with faces we wouldn't recognize. One or two, I'd say, were taken at some point during the last few laps of Lonny's time on earth. Envision the remnants of the man's life, which we have just sifted through, and the general picture will emerge—one I can hardly embellish. His beard was Abrahamic in its proportions, something that wasn't the case twenty years ago when I saw him up in Whitethorn. He came into his woolly spirit since then, unabashedly so.

Also in the folder: a snapshot of Brooke with Simon in her arms, the one I'd handed him from my wallet. It rests inside a thin mica frame, the only one so adorned. I look over at my wife, who would have already seen it, and we share this kind of weird, dissociative moment … airless, absent of sound, the meld between our fractured conceptions an almost visible, animate thing.

Why. If so, then why.

When Brooke and Mim resume their conversation, I head upstairs for a last circuit through the apartment. I mentioned earlier an absence of books on the premises: not entirely correct. There are, in the formal, card-catalog sense of the term, reference materials. Atlas, almanac, dictionary; an old single-volume encyclopedia. Also an omnibus of George Bernard Shaw plays. Fifty or so *Cartographic Journals* from decades past. That's the sum of it. I pull out the Shaw, then spend a few minutes scanning a couple dozen CDs stacked atop the bookcase. It is an odd collection: comprised almost entirely of '50s era bop, but the discs themselves are often themed, Frankenstein mashups of tracks from other legitimate recordings. *Coltrane for Lovers*—what? My only guess is that Lonny, at some juncture, cadged electrical service while he was still living on the mountain, and he celebrated by joining a CD of the month club. From where else would such desecrations originate?

Before exiting for a final time, I drop the keys to the Ranchero on top of the desk and shoot off a text to Kato telling him I've done so. It is long past ready for salvage. Brooke meets me at the foot of the stairs and informs me that Mim would like to accompany us to the beach, which, of course, is perfectly all right. Mim and I wait together while Brooke goes back up for a few moments alone, during which time I receive an abridged version of those facts she must want both of us to know: that she has been close with Lonny for over forty years; that she was never his lover; that most of his assets, including the Whitethorn property, his vehicles, and even the funds he deigned to keep in a bank account, which were minimal, were always in her name; that things were arranged this way, of course, to effectively nullify his existence in the eyes of government, of taxing authorities, of any surveilling entity—*shades of his paranoid father*, that he had erected a small art studio on her property when he moved to Shelter Cove, and by art studio I immediately understand her to mean growhouse.

She claims she was a Cistercian nun at an abbey adjoining the Whitethorn land and left the order sometime after Lonny turned up. She says this without precisely drawing a line from Lonny's arrival to her renunciation, making it difficult to reconcile with what she has already told me. In truth, it seems impossible to start at any single corner of this pastiche and make sense of it, and I decide it is too late in the day, literally and metaphorically, to even try.

Once Brooke rejoins us, I fetch Lonny's ashes from the backseat of the car, and the three of us walk slowly along the road to the lighthouse.

I wait at the base of the wood stairs while Brooke helps Mim navigate the descent. There are tidepools in the immediate vicinity, and a mother and child are poking around there, so we amble farther up the beach where the surf is moving freely and we'll be mostly unobserved. Terraced slabs of basalt extend outward from the foot of cliff, streaked white and polished smooth by the tides. A small group of seals bobs just offshore.

Brooke and Mim slip off their shoes and roll up their cuffs, then take the box with Lonny's ashes and tiptoe a few frigid steps past the waterline. This is their time, not mine, and I am content hanging back where I am.

Wearing sanitary gloves, the ones we brought from home to comb through the apartment, they scoop handfuls of ash from the box and let them fall into the outrushing waves. This takes quite a while to play out, and watching the two of them interact, overhearing an occasional word, the realization comes, and nearly knocks me over in the process, that Mim is the one grieving, Brooke the one consoling. But why wouldn't that be true? How do you mourn someone of whom you have almost no living memory, yet to whom you are so inextricably tied? Brooke would have mourned him decades ago; has mourned him in some sense her entire life. This is her release from that mourning. The dust slipping through her fingers merely perfects his insubstantiality, his diminution of self in his influence on her life. Absence of this type has no inverse, no ghostly imprint, no compensating effect. It is only absence. What was she meant to do with it? What is she meant to do with it now?

Opening my eyes to the wider seascape, I veer back to Brooke's rumination, did he "appreciate splendor," and all the evidence says he didn't, that he blew it; that he failed to recognize it when it was born to him, and how much easier can it get than that? Ironic, then, how he becomes one with it in the end, steps from his final hideaway, his spurned child to carry him there.

I walk alone back to the car and wait for Brooke and Mim to inch along. An exchange of phone numbers and addresses takes place, as it seems we'll have work to do to separate Mim's and Lonny's dealings. With daylight fading fast, I am anxious to head out, to forget this lonely place, and to put that shadowy mountain behind us. While not overly worried about the old man's warning, I'm not planning to brake for squirrels.

As we begin the twisting ride up the hill, Brooke says, "That lighthouse, did you read the plaque? They relocated it here from Cape Mendocino and flew the lantern in by helicopter."

"Must have been the ride of a lifetime for the keeper," I say.

She laughs, then settles in for the drive, and soon after closes her eyes. Three and a half hours to Crescent City and another nine tomorrow to Seattle. Her shaped life awaits her there.

GINNY'S WORLD

I find Brooke gazing out our bedroom window, running a fingertip along the curve of her ear in a gesture I have observed a thousand times. She says as I come up beside her, "We've never seen it so exposed. The barn."

As if guided by her words, a stray gust buffets a corner of its roof where the metal is no longer riveted down. It creates a percussive sound we often hear at night.

"You seem rapt," I say as she continues to stare.

"Apparently someone fitted an Andrew Wyeth into our picture window while we were away on our hike. All we're missing is the waif in the field."

"That barn is gray, I believe. If we're talking about the same painting."

She considers this and replies, "All right. A Grandma Moses, then."

"Those are two very different artists."

"Aren't they, though," she says with a small laugh.

It is near dusk and color has drained from the sky. The barn, a single-gabled affair, appears mid-collapse, as if waiting for us to turn away. The wagon door facing us lists in its frame, its crossbucks awry. What remains of its ochre paint feathers over the desiccated plank siding.

I watch a moment longer, then leave Brooke to her thoughts.

————

We awoke this morning to the thrum of a track loader leveling the untended expanse on the far side of our cedar rail fence. Twice a year I jump that fence, machete in hand, and spend hours beating back an encroachment of Himalayan blackberry, which grows rapaciously in this area. It is a dreadful job, so the arrival of heavy machinery was welcome, never mind the hour.

Before Brooke and I left for the day, I stepped outside and flagged down the operator. When land is cleared on the plateau, new development often follows, and some deeper contemplation over coffee had me wondering. As he dismounted from the cab, I recognized the adult son who lives with his mother in the modest yellow farmhouse a hundred yards or so beyond our shared property line.

Unable to retrieve his name—a sighting of him is that uncommon—I asked first after his mother, Ginny, who we had heard was in declining health. He confirmed as much, if only vaguely. Guessing at my more immediate concern, he swept his eyes over this long-forgotten back-acre of the twenty or so they still own, saying, "I rented the shovel for some other work and had an extra day before the pickup." He added with a half-smile, "I've seen you out here with the samurai sword."

I laughed off the remark, aware of how comical it must look. I might have pointed out, but didn't, that the infestation was born essentially of his own neglect. Trying to hold the line at the fence was the assignment he had left for me. Himalayan blackberry is the closest thing in nature to razor wire, setting aside its ability to autonomously grow and propagate and overrun everything in its path. It has clenched, plunging root-crowns that knot into anything that isn't bedrock and arching whorls of thorn stalks that ensnare and hold hostage competing vegetation, from mature, multi-story firs to ground cover. Appreciation of this reality came soon after our arrival here, and a regimen of manual abatement has ensued. Our politics prevent us from spraying. I have lost sleep trying to rationalize it.

The conversation with Owen, whose name Brooke reminded me of afterward, was brief and impersonal. His reference to having the loader "an extra day" was improvised, plainly. Reflecting upon it now, there was scant reason for me to take an interest. We live on land once owned by his family, as do several of our neighbors. This final piece will be shed as well. We've known that all along.

When Brooke and I returned from our day-long trek to Snoqualmie Lake, the defoliation was complete, insofar as he evidently planned to take it. The high, sprawling thicket was crushed but not removed, and the soil, and the roots it concealed, remained unscraped.

The barn was there, of course. Is there. Until today, nearly subsumed by overgrowth. The sheathing of the gable and the uppermost boards of the support walls now joined in plain view by the wreckage underneath.

It stands destitute in a razed field. A latticework of severed vines clings to the rotted wood. As I lie awake near midnight, the roof intermittently clatters in the wind, a little more resonant than before.

Returning from an appointment in the city, I discover Brooke's easel set out under our deck awning, along with its accompanying miscellanea: brushes, pie pans, palette knives, etcetera. I attempt, in the relative quiet, to sense where she might be, then retreat to the garage for a drop cloth, which I unfold beneath her work area. She'll tell me later, "I would have done that," which may be true. But I just reoiled the deck and still feel the proprietary afterglow of a recently completed task.

After pouring a gimlet for myself, I reposition one of the Adirondack chairs so I can better survey the barn. There is little doubt that the presence of the easel is attributable to it. For days, Brooke has fixated: peering out our bedroom window; gazing from our vegetable beds, hose dangling at her side; leaning against a fence post, her chin in her hands.

I search my memory: when last have her supplies found their way out of storage? She painted and drew for a time while her mother was dying. Then again as a childhood friend of hers was ushered out. Has there been another occasion since our youngest was born? Kira is a senior in college now, so more than two decades with only the rarest expense of effort.

There are practical reasons for this, certainly. Career. Motherhood. An aversion to all the solvents, spirits, noxious tints, and other constituent tools of the trade. At some point our household embarked on a quest for purity—in the air we breathe, the space we inhabit, the objects we live with or consume. Ascent to some untainted realm became the métier for Brooke, and for the kids and me by proximity. The lime juice in my glass is organic, the vodka distilled locally; the chair beneath me hewn from a reclaimed boat hull.

"When did you sneak in?" she asks, parting the leafy overhang along the walkway leading to the deck.

"No sneaking involved. Must be the lovingly restored surface underfoot."

"It does look nice," she says, then sniffs the air in mild rebuke. I used Penofin, a kind of adulterated rosewood extract, after marshalling arguments as to its durability and UV resistance. A faint, sulfurous vapor still lingers.

"I'll take that as the half-compliment it was intended to be," I say.

"I have some news, or non-news, depending on your perspective," she says, ignoring the snark. "Only the area near the barn was cleared, plus a corridor leading from the house. I was just over at the Maier's, and Vanessa and I walked the entire length of their boundary with Ginny's place."

"You can't see it all from there."

"You can see most of what we're unable to see. Enough to piece it together."

"So, what do Vanessa and Will think?"

"That they plan to use the barn again, that's all."

"It's falling apart. It would be unsafe for almost any purpose."

"We'll have to wait and see then, I guess," she says and lifts the glass from my hand, takes a cautious sip. Enough to wet her lips, nothing more.

Stepping inside, we have to navigate around the easel, but I decide that it is too soon to remark upon. Perhaps she will stay with it this time, perhaps not. No one is dying, at least. Not that I know of. In our circle, that is. Only a couple of hours ago my hematologist gave me the all-clear, or maybe I'd wonder.

Brooke muses over her subject. She constructs and deconstructs. Moves from rough sketch to formal composition to digressions in light and scale. Plays with mediums, tools, texture, dimensionality. The view alters slightly each day as the barn withers in the unfiltered sun and wind, and blackberry canes not shorn from their roots bow upward from the flattened scruff.

Three weeks have passed and new work continues to appear—if necessary, set to dry on the deck, then left inside the kitchen nook. She is aloof from us during this time. Not cold but contained; focused. This is the pattern, from experience. The aspect I always forget. That she drifts away from us for a while as she searches for balance. She has quit before she has found it, in all but distant memory.

"Start over," I say. "Tell me everything that happened."

Stifling her annoyance, she begins again, "I am upstairs. I am raising the blinds in our room. And I see him drive from the house to the barn in that farm buggy of theirs."

"It's a golf cart. With ATV tires."

"Fine, a golf cart. Does that matter?"

"Probably not," I say.

"Thank you. So, he's headed this way, and Ginny is seated beside him. But then I can't see because, you know, they're on the other side of the barn. When the cart appears again, he's alone. Driving back to the house."

"Leaving Ginny."

"Which doesn't make sense, right? Even from a distance she looked incredibly frail. So I'm watching from the window … ten minutes, twenty, maybe more. But he left her there, okay? She's out there by herself, and I'm stressing about this the entire time. So I go over the fence, go inside the barn, and there she is."

"Having tea, you said."

"Yes. No. She's in a wheelchair, pushed up to a small table. And she has dolls—two antique, porcelain dolls propped up on crates. There are cups and saucers and a teapot; a linen tablecloth. She—they—they're having a tea party. A pretend party, like you have with dolls."

"And she's talking to them? Like, a conversation?"

"Of course. Offering them cookies and such."

"Of course?"

"You have a daughter, Jeff, correct? I'll introduce her to you the next time she's home. She was a little girl just a few years ago."

"All right, all right ..."

"And so I ask Ginny if I can join her, and she says, 'Please do.' And she offers me tea, and it goes on from there. Like I am a friend she has invited or another of her dolls."

"Did she recognize you?" I ask. "I mean, when she was still getting around, we saw quite a bit of her."

"I'm sure she didn't. I just never had that feeling. And then Owen came back, maybe a half-hour after I sat down. He glanced at me but didn't say anything. He lifted Ginny out of the chair, really gently, and carried her to the buggy ... she's a leaf now, Jeff. I could have carried her. And then they're gone, and then, ah ... I don't know ... I just don't ..."

She gazes past me, lost in a way she so rarely is. I offer my shoulder and she accepts it, but I have the sense that she's hardly there. It's as if our view, our *Wyeth*, has become animate and drawn her in. Made her a part of its blighted tableau. Perhaps this is the reason, the essential reason, she has given up art in the past. She finds herself vanishing into her subject ... her subject being death, disintegration, erasure. The certainty that we have arrived there again is the tension in our embrace.

———

The scene repeats itself the following afternoon and the next one as well. Brooke goes over the fence each time. Ginny would play there as a child, it seems, inside the red barn. In the slow peeling-away of her memory, she has alighted there once more.

There will be no fourth day, as it happens. We learn, in the course of the month, of a home-hospice arrangement. Help is offered, flowers sent, meals brought to the door. The Maiers take the lead. It proves necessary for only a short while. Owen remains a specter throughout.

Before long, the property is sold, all twenty acres. The structures are dismantled; the land contoured and subdivided. Foundations are poured and houses framed. Brooke records the progression. She doesn't paint every day, but the intent is there. We begin to talk about a studio.

Two summers on, we have several new neighbors. Young families with tots and grade-schoolers. While idling on the deck one day, we spy a small figure in the narrow greenbelt that now skirts our backyard. The county, we were surprised to discover, owns an easement along the dividing line and prevented the developer from grading right up to the fence.

I call it a greenbelt, but, of course, it's a bramble of blackberry and strangled seedlings and very little else. We watch as this slight, darting imp, the child of one of the newcomers, moves from stalk to stalk, carefully plucking among the thorns. He sees us and grins, his chin smudged purple. The berries are dark and sweet right now, and we have enjoyed a good many ourselves.

It is neither here nor there, how things have settled out. Benign neglect has given way to contrived order; still life to movement and motif. The field itself was the canvas

in this respect, and in the playfulness of a child we can
admire the craft. In turn, we're the preserved image now.
The known world the boy sees when he glances this way.
We do what we can about the upkeep.

209

MEDITATIONS IN
GUARDED ACKNOWLEDGMENT

AN INSTINCT FOR MOVEMENT

Decades ago, on a church parking lot in the Brandy-wine Hundred district north of Wilmington, a street hockey game was convened on Halloween day between the Cardiff and Woodbine subdivisions. It would be an uneven match, as Cardiff was by far the smaller of the two communities and couldn't match the depth, speed, and physical stature of the horde mustered by Woodbine.

Seconds after the puck dropped, the rout was on, and with the outcome never in doubt, the game inside the game took shape. The blindside checking, the ankle swatting, the jabs to the sternum and kidneys. Cardiff scrapped and returned fire, but there was an aspect of malevolence bred into the Woodbine lot which, when paired with their brawn and shaved stick blades, left the Cardiff boys in a bad way.

In the closing minutes of the game, a squat, crude punk named Frankie White, minding goal for Woodbine, spied a rival player floating alone outside a scrum near the centerline. It was the Alexander kid who, in most prior shared contexts, had remained all but invisible to him. Moments earlier, that kid gathered in a stray carom and flicked it between the pudge-goalie's thighs, grazing his unprotected tool kit on its way to the back of the net. White was still fuming over the loss of his shutout, and a lethal current of arousal radiated up from his singed nut hairs.

From a distance of some thirty feet, and with his stick handle braced horizontally in front of him, White took aim at his idling opponent. In the seconds before the cross-check arrived, Alexander, seasoned from years of lawless sandlot games in all manner of sports, teased out an errant wisp of danger from the cool October air. The instinct for movement came too late. The birchwood shaft cratered into his thoracic vertebrae, buckling his knees, splaying his arms, and snapping his head backward. The recoil propelled him face-first to the asphalt, where he lay concussed and spouting blood from his mouth and flagrantly broken nose.

Enraged, an until-then generally disinterested recruit to the Cardiff side—they often didn't have enough bodies to field a team and would round up mercenaries from nearby unincorporated housing tracts—instantly jumped the crazed, cheap-shot Woodbiner. White's teammates, reluctant to come to his aid out of their own disregard for him, and wary of, or perhaps captivated by, the adrenaline-fueled fury on display, allowed the pummeling to seek its natural end.

At some point, the crumpled, immediately forgotten Alexander boy, while struggling and failing to get to his feet, which he couldn't yet establish clear, lineal contact with, glanced over and caught sight of the proceedings through a swarm of legs and stick shafts. Lifting his head, he took note of the figure doling out justice on his behalf. Not a friend. Not a boy he knew well. A better liked, higher ranked kid in the unstable but always operational hierarchy among area middle-school males.

He understood, even through his haze, that the vengeance being wrought had as much or more to do with the accumulated humiliation of the full hour that had just passed and the boy's anger at being drawn into it. Still, a hard seed of respect travelled upstream through his veins and settled deep in his core. A realignment was taking place; a new vector mapped between two remote satellites in their malign, chaotic, adolescent world.

In the moment before he passed out, which he felt an overwhelming desire to do, Alexander allowed his eyes to drift, locate those of Frankie White, whose head presently was being palmed into the blacktop. He wondered, in those fluttering seconds, if what he was seeing was real: the glee, the jagged-toothed grin, the hollow sockets, the preposterously fat, orange face; the flames licking from inside. He tried to laugh, but it hurt, and he puked himself unconscious.

It would be going too far to say they became friends, the boy who was knocked flat and the brawler who sprang to his defense. The first was a loner and the second was a jock, embedded deep in the jock milieu. If they encountered each other at school, they might nod or exchange a word, but that didn't happen often. There was no common plane on which they roamed.

The following summer, the dynamic shifted, as both were the sons of small-time contractors—electrical in the case of Alexander, plumbing for the other boy, Menotti. Long yoked to their families' businesses, despite their youth, they began to run into each other on job sites or at the supply house. Away from the burdens of cliques and hallway rule, a certain affinity was able to take hold.

Years would pass in this way: ignoring each other for nine months, drawing closer for three. Closer, in this case, meaning something beyond casual indifference.

Finding themselves alone one morning doing pre-structural work on a commercial lot, Alexander noticed Menotti lagging, unable to keep himself upright. This wasn't without context. Menotti, by then, had traded athletics for drugs, at times to conspicuous effect. Alexander was a user too, but, as before, he felt himself an amateur, a scrub player when compared to Menotti and his now formidable credentials as a stoner.

He walked over to where Menotti knelt amid a network of trenches, his face in his hands.

"Nick," he called out, unsure if he was heard or if Menotti was even awake. He gazed awhile at the clean, graded furrows cut into the soil. They must have used a Ditch Witch, he thought, more than a little enviously. His own father never sprang for such luxuries.

Eventually Menotti bobbed up, saying, "I'll catch no end of shit if I don't get this laid out." He gestured faintly toward a stack of plastic pipe before launching into a coughing jag and curling back into himself.

Alexander gathered up several drawings lying loose near his feet and leafed through them. Isometric drawings, sketched by hand. The top one appeared to correspond to the general area where they—or rather he—now stood.

"This looks pretty straightforward," he said, keeping his tone flat, unsure if the encouragement would be welcome. Menotti may have nodded or may not have—it was difficult to say what was or wasn't a voluntary movement at that point. Alexander fetched a Coke from his mini-cooler and handed it down to him, then watched as he rolled the can along his neck and forehead before opening it with some effort.

There was an aspect to this situation that Alexander reflexively understood: being dropped off at a site by the crew leaders, with an impossible amount of work to do or a task they knew was out of his range. The senior guys loved it when the boss's son fucked up, and they looked for their chances. He hated giving them the satisfaction, and it was this, as much as anything, that had compelled him to learn and to work fast.

He peered again at the drawings, shook his head, spat over his shoulder. Electricians, as a rule, looked down on plumbers, and though he didn't fully understand why, he had internalized the sentiment. Still, on occasion, he found himself consigned to such work and had picked up enough to cheat.

"I can help you with this," he said, realizing full well he would suffer his own hailstorm of grief should his own work not get done.

It was a punishment he was willing to abide. Three years he had waited for a chance to repay a debt, and now that chance had arrived. The time and circumstances were of Menotti's blind choosing: a shadeless dirt lot off Basin Road in New Castle; an oppressive mid-August day; the air and ground quaking every few minutes from a takeoff or landing at the adjoining municipal airport.

Working side by side for hours on end, and with the sun flaming down and bronzing their shirtless backs, they built up the gravel bed, cut and laid the PVC, primed the pipe ends, and dry-set the fittings and risers. Reviving by fits and starts, Menotti was a whirlwind by the finish, and the results of his and Alexander's labor, while almost certainly out of spec, did not look awful. Or so they agreed. At a minimum, passed the unspoken thought between them, their handiwork would satisfy whatever base expectations were there when Menotti was rolled out of a truck six hours before, drooling and near insensate.

Happy and exhausted, they lay sprawled at the end of the day on what remained of the gravel pile, passing a joint, monitoring the air traffic, warm flakes of quarry rock trickling along their spines. Soon their respective tormentors would roll up in panel trucks and carry them their separate ways. Apropos of nothing they had discussed until then, and after a heroically long belch, Menotti said idly, "This is my last summer doing this. I'm taking off after we graduate."

Unsure if this should matter to him, and feeling no urgency to decide, Alexander set his mind adrift. A vintage aluminum turboprop swooped low overhead, rivets gleaming, gearbox whining. A woman in a white headscarf pushed a stroller along the roadside, a second child poking along behind her. His eyes beginning to close, he heard Menotti say, "You?"

"Sorry?" he said, thinking he had missed something.

"Your plans, what are they? College, your dad's business—what?"

"One of those two," he was slow to reply, lucky to have found even those simple words. Never before had Menotti expressed any real curiosity about his life. He marveled over this breakthrough until Menotti spoke again, "He's an asshole, isn't he?"

"My dad?"

"I've seen him in action. Around you, anyway."

"Oh …"

"Mine isn't. I just hate plumbing. The idea that this is what I'm meant to do."

"Where are you planning to go?" he asked, feeling suddenly that it was important to know.

"Not sure yet," Menotti replied, laughing. "Got any ideas? It has to be far."

Alexander laughed too, but only as a cover for the obvious. That he had no ideas. No ideas and no plans. Not for himself and not for anyone else. He dreaded his inheritance no less than Menotti dreaded his, he was sure, and likely for grimmer, more persuasive reasons. But he could only admire the resolve to disown it.

Moments later, Menotti was off, a trail of exhaust and clodded dirt spewing in his wake. Alexander pinched away the fizzled joint, gathered his things, and waited. Bored, he crouched over one of the vertical pipe stubs, covered the opening with his hands and mouth, and blew. After a few tries, he hit on a certain vibrating bass note, one he could sustain and modulate. Like the low throb of a didgeridoo or a drone string plucked over a hollow gourd.

There's a plan, he thought, a little too late for sharing, but at least it finally came, and it even carried a whiff of adventure … *head for the Southern Hemisphere, listen for ancient sounds, surf the desert wind …*

"Sure you will," he said to nothing and to no one, giving it the consideration it was due and more or less speaking both for himself and for Menotti.

There were times during their senior year when Menotti could be found on school grounds, though only for sure if he had business to take care of. In addition to moving increasing quantities of drugs, he had added bookmaking to his portfolio, ostensibly as an intermediary. Each week, he distributed parlay cards on the day the point spreads were set, collected the wagers, and ran the cash to a local agent. Or so it was commonly understood.

In fact, at some point, no one knew exactly when, he began running the book, or part of the book, himself; this, after observing that the bets were small—rarely more than ten dollars a week from any single kid—and that almost everyone lost. Backstopping the action on his own account, for a pool typically comprised of his most idiotic classmates, seemed like easy money.

This worked fine for a while. The gross wasn't as good as with weed and quaaludes, but the hassle quotient was far lower: no upfront capital, no supply chain, no physical inventory, no quality control issues. So what if he had to pay out on a winner every couple of weeks. He was way ahead and felt confident he would remain so.

Alexander steered clear of all this, though not out of probity or restraint. His modest requirements for bud were satisfied by an older cousin, and he confined his wagering to the thoroughbreds at the local raceway when it opened in June. It was a good way to bracket his risk: the season ran through summer and corresponded to when he actually had money in his pocket, working full time for his father. The proximity to the action; the cerebral, almost sensory aspects of handicapping; the sound and smell and anticipation as the horses broke and jostled and sprinted free—all of it was more appealing than trying to win four-for-fours while betting on teams you couldn't care less about playing games you'd never see.

Come Super Bowl week, upon hearing that Menotti was banking on a last, big take for the year, and despite his prior demurrals, Alexander feared he might be lassoed in, and he was. Cornered in a stairwell between classes, he slipped Menotti a twenty and took the underdog with points, while parlaying the over on each quarter. It was a ridiculous bet, yet he scarcely had time to consider it.

"Good play," Menotti said with almost laughable disinterest, then cuffed him on the shoulders and began to stroll away.

Alexander took a step in the same direction, hand extended, the escape of the banknote still drafting over his fingertips. The moment felt familiar to him in some way … the low voltage of recovered instinct; an almost tactile sense of imminence. He would always have difficulty saying no to Menotti, he realized, yet he gleaned in that instant that it would soon cease to matter. His debt was settled, their paths were diverging. The before and after of their lives was only months away.

As Menotti dropped down the stairs, Alexander called to him, spurred by a dying impulse, yet his voice clear and connotative enough to be both heard and understood—he said, "Know where you're going yet, Nick?" But Menotti was lost in thought, or computations, and didn't glance up, didn't break stride, offered no acknowledgement at all.

When, the following week, his longshot having come in, Alexander was handed back his twenty by a third party saying Menotti failed to lay off the risk in time, he felt fully returned to himself; to the annihilating moment of impact; his scaffolding blown nearly in half; his premonition rewarded if his luck was not. This lie was born years ago. Born on a church parking lot a half-mile away. The several hundred dollars forgone was both its expression and its negation. A discounting of value to its intrinsic state.

Alexander found his way to Menotti's locker, wrote "Australia" across the face of the twenty, and poked it through the door vent. Then he skipped his last class and walked home. He would have to wait until late spring, but he'd win it back at the raceway, easy.

He located his father in the dining hall, jawing with another graybeard. It was quarter past 6:00 p.m., the room all but cleared out, a few stragglers killing time before the slow shuffle back to their apartments. The staff worked around them, clearing tables, vacuuming, setting out napkins and flatware for the next meal.

As always, he was introduced with a tag line, one of several his father would use, "My son, the left coaster," *the blue stater, the long loster, the stay away,* and so forth, most of which were true, even literal, while remaining faithful to their pejorative intent. He had stopped taking the bait decades before.

He shook hands with his father's companion and pulled up a chair. They rarely stood on ceremony, he and his father, and these arrivals, often years apart, were meditations in guarded acknowledgment. Gus, the other resident, seemed aggrieved by this, but he caught himself quickly, and in no time it was just two aged bullshitters off on another spiel. They were waxing about the old days, which were likely the only days they could safely account for, though in this case it became clear that there was actual shared history involved. The son, no youth himself, listened as the talk careered between umbrage, mockery, ribald humor, fleeting agreement, and, on more than one occasion, sheer loss of the thread.

He wasn't bored—far from it. The common ground they were plowing was also, to an extent, his own and dated to his father's near lifetime in the trades and, evidently, Gus's as well. An appreciable chunk of that he had lived through, though just barely. If he sat there and minded the occasional urge to correct them, he told himself, he might be able to get through this.

"Can I pour you some decaf?" came the voice of a cherub in a white shirt and black apron.

"Yes, please," he said, vastly understating both his need for a calmative and his appreciation for the interruption. She proceeded to loiter at the table and trade banter and innuendo with the old men.

As this quaint transaction unfolded, his attention came to rest on the illuminated ceramic pumpkin situated in front of him. There was one on each table, along with a small arrangement of flint corn, and a life-size cardboard skeleton dangling from the drop ceiling in the middle of the room. He'd noticed similar things on prior visits: the common areas spruced up with themed or seasonal decorations. In this instance, he questioned the wisdom: all good intentions aside, a certain climate of horror was endemic to such places and hardly needed accessorizing. At least this wasn't the lost-souls wing. The residents here still had possession of themselves, more or less.

Continuing to gaze at the pumpkin, yet now, somehow, with a kind of sidelong recognition, and guessing at the gist of what he was about to find out, he said to the foul-mouthed but essentially kind elderly gentleman seated across from him, "What was your last name again?"

"That's Gus," his father scolded him. "Gus Menotti. You remember: Menotti's Plumbing? We worked a hundred jobs together and they screwed up every time."

They stared at him, these two enfeebled lions, seeking affirmation, yearning to see something register. Such were the moments, he had come to learn, when we disappoint our forebears most: when we force them, intentionally or not, to confront the dissolution of their own history; how none of it will be remembered, none of it will be real, in due time. Of course, he did remember, but he couldn't, in any event, give them the satisfaction. One thing would lead to another, wouldn't it? He imagined his name being mentioned, the inevitable blank being drawn. A minor invalidation of his own.

He steered the conversation instead to Gus's family and in this way learned that his only son, "Nicky," ran a catering business in L.A., "high class all the way," been out there forever, wife, children, house in Santa Monica, and, oh, by the by, "You didn't happen to know him, did you? You look about the same age."

He nearly laughed out loud at the question, though much of that was relief—relief that Menotti hadn't wandered off a cliff or spent his adult life in the crowbar hotel, possibilities he had entertained from time to time and not without justification.

"No, I can't say I knew him," he replied, glad he didn't have to lie, though a little sorry for having spoiled the party.

WAVEFORMS

Morning Traffic Report

Two boys dart though through a field surrounding a radio tower. They scrabble over its wire fence and pick up a rising dirt path beaten to hardpan by thousands of prior shortcutters. Quieted by their nerves, they eye a brick hub-and-spoke building situated at the top of the incline. Virtue will soon accrue to this day, their first of fourth grade, but they can't see their way clear to that yet.

Short of their destination, one of the two youths, Jeffrey Alexander, senses an approach from behind and to his right. He reacts in time to plant a leg behind his assailant's lead foot and leverages him to the ground. It's Ricky Reese, a classmate he fell out with the year before, welcoming him back to the fray. Reese bucks him off, and they wrestle on the grass until a shout from an adult breaks them apart.

Alexander snatches up his pack and backs away toward his companion, Jaime—a new kid who, to his credit, didn't bolt at the sign of trouble. Reese, after a moment of indecision, peels off, spitting invective as he goes. This won't be the end of it.

The boys resume their climb, and as they approach the narrow drive leading to the staff parking lot, a yellow

T-top Corvette eases by, its heartbeat drumming through the soles of their sneakers. The two have bonded over cool cars, and they gaze in admiration at the low slink of the throaty, gleaming machine.

In no hurry to take their final few steps toward institutional confinement, they track the Corvette as it throttles to a stop, then drop their packs in wonder as a lissome blonde in an orange leather skirt unfolds from behind the wheel and strolls toward the faculty entrance. She pauses yards away from them and fixes her lively eyes upon the stunned Alexander boy.

"School hasn't even started yet and look at you," she says with a smile and a wave before disappearing through the metal door. The grass in his hair, the dirt pasted to his shirt, the freshly opened patch in his jeans—none of it, for the boy, connects to her words, only the heat that rockets through him when she speaks them. Like a freak pulse from the giant signal tower behind him.

It is a premonitory feeling. One he'll recognize and make sense of in the decade to come, but which, for a nine-year-old, is unnaturally ahead of schedule.

Presently the boys enter their new classroom. There they encounter the same unearthly vision, one Caroline Trice, their teacher and inamorata for the fall and spring terms. Thus begins their most attentive year of school at any level and, for Alexander, the enshrining of a memory from a childhood in Delaware he'll mostly wish he could forget.

By day's end, others have staked a claim to the new kid, and Alexander is left to walk home alone. Lost inside himself, his defenses down, he is once again ambushed by Ricky Reese, and this time he eats his ration of sod. The taste is somehow less sour, the subjugation less complete, than it might otherwise have been.

He gathers himself up from the ground and continues on his way: over the perimeter fence, under the guy wires, across the gated road leading to the tower base and station building. As he slips into the woods toward his home, he snaps off a punk from a dead sapling and gnaws on it, thinking.

More Music More Music

A Coke, two hard boiled eggs, a dozen or so pretzel rods, and what else? His appetite, a kinetic force inside him as he enters his middle teens. A conveyor for beanpole growth and unchained juvenility.

He ponders the open refrigerator, then fetches a can of spaghetti from the pantry. He fits it against the electric opener and scores off the lid.

Leaning against the counter, eating straight from the can, he hears a voice. But his brother is up the street and his parents are at work. He creeps toward the hallway and the voice dissipates. Retracing his steps, he hears it anew. No. He hears music. Singing.

He repeats this a second and third time. Same result. He glances up at the air register and wonders if it is carrying the sound, but, again, he is the only one home. Raising the window over the sink, he notices movement on the far creekbank: Jaime Livingston and two other boys skirting the wooded property line. Jaime holds a Daisy air rifle—he would recognize it at any distance. But the voice he hears—it is once again a voice, a speaking voice, not a song—is not Jaime's; not either of the boys' with him.

Jaime flicks his gaze toward the house. They were pals once, he and Jaime. One summer, years ago. They are not necessarily at odds now, just different circles. Jaime with the farm boys, he with the outcasts. Their parents are friends still.

He shuts the window and closes his eyes, concentrates. Attempts to trace the disembodied sound. When he peers out, he sees—he is inches away from—the can opener. He distinctly hears the call letters announced for the AM station behind the woods. Then another song, a softie, which is all they ever play. Turning again toward the window, he rests his eyes upon the lattice tower, its upper section rising over the treetops. A few hundred yards away at most. The glint from its lantern nearly erased by the slanting sunlight. A moment later, the noise cuts out.

When his father returns home, he violates his own code, learned at great cost: keep your head down; never initiate; one-word answers; mockery is your defense if you need it. It has spared him untold grief and consoled him when it hasn't. But his father is an electrician, was a shipboard radio tech in the Navy. He'll know.

"I heard WDEL through the can opener."

His father stares at him. Stares as if to say, *Everything else over these last fourteen years and now this.*

"It played a song," he tells him. "I heard it. How does that happen."

And then there is a shift. One he wouldn't understand. That throws him off-center. His father's brow unstitches, his jaw relaxes. A tenuous light arcs in his eyes; behind his eyes; deep, yet visible. A father reminded of a fleeting time, before he raised his hand against his child. When some quaint notion of a son seeking wisdom and a father passing it along hadn't been so thoroughly disabused.

Disoriented, this boy, Jeffrey Alexander, he takes in but cannot fully assemble, in the aftermath, what his father has said: the Blaw-Knox tower design; the five-kilowatt signal; modulated waveforms; an oscillating metal vibrating the air; the presence of a magnet and a diode. He has the pieces but not the comprehension … other than it is possible. It may have happened. He is in his right mind, inasmuch as he ever has been.

Which will have to be enough. He won't dare ask again.

That Ball is Outta Here

It is October of 1993. An early-twentieth-century Jewish émigré from the eastern Pale is asleep on a recliner inside his apartment off Foulk Road in North Wilmington. The kitchen radio is on, a vintage tabletop Silvertone he has had restored on more than a few occasions. On the sofa next to him, his adult grandson, Jeffrey, visiting from California where he has lived for some years, has just opened his eyes. The younger man yawns, checks his watch, then refocuses his attention on the broadcast. The game, he realizes, is now in the ninth inning, and the Phillies have somehow taken the lead. There are two men on base, one out, and the reliever nicknamed "Wild Thing" is on the mound. Retire this batter and one more and the series goes to game seven. Allow the baserunners to score and the season is over.

Staring at the old, AM-only receiver, a tube model with an umber, Bakelite shell, the grandson surmises he is among the very few people in the Delaware Valley experiencing this moment purely through audio … though, perhaps, some who are watching have turned away. Those with a refined appreciation of local lore, certainly.

On a 2-2 count, and with the play-by-play man narrating over the roar of crowd, the Phillies' daredevil closer offers up a gopher ball to the opposing team's big bat, promptly ending the game and the series. History, once again, is served.

Jeffrey looks over at his grandfather, whose head is canted to one shoulder. He stands and stretches, then steps over to a gateleg table pushed against a wall in the kitchenette. He lingers over the radio as the announcer, in his slow, baritone drawl, deftly compresses the five stages of grief into a few moments of postmortem reverie.

After the handoff to the local station, he turns off the radio, then leans over the sink and splashes his face with water. He takes an afghan from the back of the sofa and lays it gently across his Zayde's chest and legs. He often sleeps on the recliner, and it is approaching midnight, so he wouldn't think to wake him.

Before leaving, he unplugs the space heater, dims the floor lamp, then kisses his grandfather lightly on the forehead. He pauses on the front stoop and reflects on whether he'll see him again. He is still strong, still sharp, but it is far from a sure thing. On the drive to the airport to catch his red-eye, he can't find anything on the dial he wants to listen to, so he lets his mind wander.

From pogroms as a child to baseball as a nonagenarian, what wind takes you there …

———

Night Caller

Jeffrey Alexander, no longer a youth nor a young man, yet with conflict still to resolve, steps outside for air and decides to make a circuit of the building he has just exited. His brother hadn't bothered to tell him, only provided the facility name and street address: their primary school, now a convalescent home. All but one of its wings, that is. The last is a hospice. Inside, his father parachutes through the final stages of his descent. Tomorrow or the next day, at the latest.

He lingers near a bench on the east side of the grounds and gazes over the empty space toward the tower array. Not one but three now … *or has it always been so.* An aureole glows at the top of each mast, an aviation lamp at its center. It is a damp, chilly night, but he is held still by the vision. The same he was rarely out of sight of through nearly all his early life.

A woman emerges from a service door and asks if he is all right. Taking him for a grieving relative, he supposes. Is that what he is? It will take some time to know.

They begin to chat, and it arises that she volunteers at the hospice once a month and has done so since her aunt died there a year ago. Also that she is employed at the radio station, which, unexplainably, delights him.

"I am wholly unprepared for this conversation," he tells her, unable to suppress a laugh.

"Why so?"

"You have to understand, that tower … the main tower … it was the homing beacon of my childhood. I could see it while lying in bed. I cut through that field a million times, often while being chased. I climbed every tree in the woods behind it. There are … there are so many questions, and I can't think of a single one right now."

"You might know more than I do," she says, laughing right along. "I have only worked there a few years."

"Once—once, I heard a song through our can opener. 'Take a Letter Maria.' Then it kept happening. The phone, a box fan. The tonearm on my record player. I can't remember what else."

"Ah, yes. Music. There is such a thing, isn't there? Those were the old, old days for AM, before 24/7 outrage programming. And religion on Sundays, of course, though the distinction isn't always obvious. But not to complain, I have a job in broadcasting, right?"

He throws back his head and says, "I'm ready to bust up again, but this isn't the place for it, is it?"

"This is exactly the place for it," she says, and he can already recite the rest: that everyone needs a release at such times, the swings in emotion are natural, and so on. He kicks himself for giving her the opening and instantly feels the need to stamp out any vague notions she might have about his fragile state of mind. His father dying, it's not like that for him. Though he can't say precisely what it is like.

"It makes you wonder, with all the ancients here," he says. "The pacemakers. The hearing aids. The steel hip joints. The dental implants. They're walking antennae. If they weren't hearing voices before they got here, they must be now."

"You forgot the dipole metal walkers."

"That's right! A perfect design."

She says she needs to be on her way and offers him her sympathies, a hair premature and unwanted besides.

He thanks her for her kindness. As she strolls toward her car, something about the way she carries herself, and her irreverent charm, along with this piercing sense of where he is standing …

She's what, twenty years younger than he is? Time, flipped on its axis somehow. She could be Caroline Trice, she is that arresting, though with a unity of form all her own. Of course, he can name his impulses now, and the intensity with which they arrive isn't quite as riotous, so that's progress on both counts, he supposes. Still, he can feel the buzz, he can hear the music, it is familiar, it is directional, and he has learned to listen for the grace notes at the most unlikely of times.

Before heading back inside, where his tyrant father cranes for his last wisps of air, he looks up again at the towers, at the illuminated station building at their base. Somewhere in there, he allows himself to imagine, it is all stored on a console, the entire eighteen-plus years. He could call in one night and have them play it back for him, it would fill in the gaps, he could get his stories straight, maybe understand a little better how he has arrived at such a moment, or any moment, really.

He wonders if Jaime is still around, or Ricky Reese, or any of his other sometime-friends, sometime-nemeses. Or, like him, did they stumble out of signal range and keep going, as far away as they could, in his case to the opposite coast where the distances are greater, the mountains higher, and it is easier to escape the noise. His brother, who stayed, would know. They'll have all night to compare notes.

ACKNOWLEDGMENTS

Grateful acknowledgment to the publications in which the following stories first appeared:

"Afterglow", *Chicago Quarterly Review*

"Wayfinder", *Santa Monica Review*

"No Living Memory", *Santa Monica Review*

"Waveforms", *Chicago Quarterly Review*

"An Instinct for Movement", *Santa Monica Review*

"Ginny's World", *Cirque*

"Field Notes from the Spring Bird Census", *Santa Monica Review*

"Surface to Air", *Santa Monica Review*

"An Undignified Name for a Horse" (originally published under the title "The Only Revenge Available"), *West Branch*

Thank you especially to Andrew Tonkovich, who time and again has found space for my work in *Santa Monica Review*.

All respect and gratitude to the editing and creative teams at Cornerstone Press, including Brett Hill, Ellie Atkinson, Carolyn Czerwinski, Sthefanie Padilla, Ava

Willett, and Sophie McPherson. And profound thanks to Dr. Ross K. Tangedal, who guided *An Instinct for Movement* from acquisition to publication.

Nearly all the stories in this collection first passed the eyes of my critique group, cast apart by the pandemic. Their insights were invaluable, and their names must be credited here: Bill Eisele, Zach Miller, Erika Sanders, and Lois Taylor. Similar thanks are extended to Molly Ringle and Julie Deutscher.

This day might never have come if not for the unending encouragement of my family, both near and far, but especially Clara Mattes, Daniel Mattes, and Dr. Nathan Simon. And to Katherine, Simon, and Kira: thank you for the stolen time and attention to pursue my dream.

Michael Mattes grew up in Delaware and later spent time in San Francisco, Chicago, and the Desert Southwest. His fiction has appeared in *Santa Monica Review, Chicago Quarterly Review, World Literature Today, West Branch, Cirque,* and elsewhere. He and his family now call western Washington home and hope to never leave. More at msmattes.wordpress.com.

www.ingramcontent.com/pod-product-compliance
Lightning Source LLC
Chambersburg PA
CBHW032245310726
48973CB00008B/2305